A hundred shades of black

McCarter retrieved his lighter and ignited it. Flickering shadows danced on the bare walls and floor. Against the back wall was the outline of another door. No doorknob or handle marred its smooth surface.

"Hey!" shouted the terrorist from the corridor. "Are you still there? Ha! Of course you are. But not for long."

McCarter heard it then—the oversize door at the rear sliding open. He braced himself, expecting a hail of bullets.

All he got was heavy breathing. Unable to resist, he flicked on the lighter again.

"Bloody hell."

Filling the doorway was a creature out of a nightmare. The meanest-looking bull he had ever seen, its eyes twin pools of red-reflected hate.

"There's a good boy," McCarter said.

The great beast snorted, its horns impaling the air. Then a thousand pounds of fury hurtled at McCarter.

Mack Bolan's
PHOENIX FORCE

PHOENIX FORCE

Fair Game

Gar Wilson

A GOLD EAGLE BOOK FROM
WORLDWIDE

TORONTO • NEW YORK • LONDON • PARIS
AMSTERDAM • STOCKHOLM • HAMBURG
ATHENS • MILAN • TOKYO • SYDNEY

First edition November 1987

ISBN 0-373-61332-6

Special thanks and acknowledgment to
Paul Glen Neuman for his contribution to this work.

Printed in Canada

Prologue

Not all of the tourists brought cameras.

Fifty-eight passengers rode the Transcantabrico—Spain's answer to the Orient Express. Combining creature comforts of a modern age, without sacrificing the character of a bygone era, the Transcantabrico consisted of four sleeping cars, four salon cars and a club car. All the train's cars were vintage 1920s, paneled in rich dark mahogany and plushly furnished throughout.

During its five-month season, which lasted from June to October, the Transcantabrico began its journey in the city of León, the former Roman legion camp that later became a refuge for Christians under Muslim rule. From León the train traveled northeast to the resort city of Santander on the Bay of Biscay, then went west along the Cantabrian coast toward the northwest corner of Spain, where it stopped in El Ferrol. On alternating weeks, the seven-day excursion began in El Ferrol and ended in León.

Marianne Hanfield, the daughter of a U.S. senator, didn't like trains as a rule. A long bumpy ride in a cramped uncomfortable seat, while mile after mile of uninteresting scenery crawled by, wasn't her idea of a good time, let alone a vacation worth paying for.

She'd take a first-class seat on a jumbo jet any day. To Marianne, nothing beat flying; it was the only way to travel from point A to point B without having to endure the clickety-clack monotony of riding the rails.

That was why, forty-eight hours into the family holiday she was taking with her daughter and son, Marianne was pleasantly surprised to discover that she was actually enjoying herself. The first clue that her preconceptions regarding train travel were due for a major shakeup had come shortly after the Transcantabrico's departure from León, when the passengers were treated to complimentary sherry, salted almonds and potato chips.

This initial get-together served as an icebreaker for everyone, and before too long most of the vacationers were behaving as though they had known one another for years. Nor was this feeling of friendliness dispelled after day settled into night and it was time to turn in.

Half expecting that she and her children would be forced to sleep standing up, Marianne found their accommodations more than adequate. Although not much larger than four feet by six feet, their compartment consisted of bunk beds, several tiny drawers, three clothes hooks and a medicine cabinet. A small closet reserved for their belongings was in the hall outside their compartment, as were separate shower and toilet facilities that they shared with fifteen other tourists occupying their sleeping car.

Midday and evening meals were eaten in various *mesones*, as the restaurants of northern Spain were often called. With fare that had already included fresh mountain trout, plus a snack of blue Cabrales cheese served with cider, everyone eagerly awaited the next culinary adventure on the train's ambitious schedule.

Traveling the narrow-gauge rails enabled the Transcantabrico to visit isolated crannies of Spanish landscape that would otherwise pass unnoticed. Riding time between stops rarely exceeded two hours at a stretch, and a bus accompanied the train for excursions beyond the limits of the tracks.

Sitting at a table in the club car, absently watching the bus keep pace with the train, Marianne turned away from the window at the sound of her daughter's voice.

"I'm sorry, dear," the woman said. "You were saying?"

Jessica Hanfield smiled at her brother, Ron, who was sitting next to her, then repeated to her mother, "I said, 'It looks to me like you're daydreaming.'"

"Me? Never, dear." She indicated the bus outside. "I was just wondering where the bus would be taking us for lunch today."

"Well, wherever it is," Ron Hanfield offered, "I'm sure we'll like it. Any place that hasn't been invaded by golden arches and processed chicken chunks can't be all bad. So far, this vacation has proved a winner all the way."

When the boy's mother did not respond immediately, his sister promptly added, "Admit it, Mom. I know Ron and I are responsible for talking you into taking this vacation, but now that you're finally on it, aren't you having even a little bit of fun?"

"Of course I am, Jessica. And you and Ron are to be congratulated. If the rest of our ride to El Ferrol is as interesting and peaceful as it has been up to now, then I wouldn't be surprised if this didn't turn out to be the best vacation I've ever been on."

Ron gestured to the numerous other passengers assembled in the club car. "Having such nice people to travel with makes all the difference in the world."

Jessica giggled. "I don't suppose that has anything to do with the fact that one of those 'nice' people happens to be a cute young redhead from Scotland?"

"Hey!" Ron protested. "I didn't see you looking the other way when that guy from Italy started giving you the eye."

"That's different," Jessica said. "Tony's never met a girl from America before."

"Ha! That's what he says."

"Children," Marianne interrupted, amused that her two teenagers should be carrying on so. "I'm sure Tony's intentions toward Jessica are just as sincere as Ron's are to Linda."

Now it was Jessica's turn to laugh.

There was an organ nestled in one corner at the far end of the club car, and, as Marianne and her children continued their conversation, an organist took a seat at the keyboard and began to play. The song was a Spanish tune unfamiliar to the three Americans, but the lively rhythm and lilting melody soon had their toes tapping in time to the music.

As the music continued, the more venturesome passengers unashamedly started to sing. Others, less bold, compromised by clapping their hands and lah-dee-dahing their way through the number. Even Jessica and Ron, Marianne noted, were not immune to the infectious beat of the song.

Flipping open her copy of the Transcantabrico's weeklong itinerary, Marianne read the description of events waiting for them in the coastal city of Santander. There they would have a free evening to explore the fishermen's quarter, the resort's casino, or to visit anywhere their curiosity led them.

Marianne found the prospect of going to the casino intriguing, but wondered what she would do with her children if she decided to go. Jessica was fifteen. Ron was two years older. They were hardly babies, yet Marianne still found it difficult to accept that they were growing up. Could she risk leaving them unchaperoned for an hour or so? Of course, now that she thought about it, what with Tony from Italy and Linda from Scotland, her son and daughter might welcome a chance for some free time of their own.

The train slowly crested the top of a hill, puffing and chugging its way over a ridge that was carpeted with yellow flowers. The organist finished the first song and, to the accompaniment of well-deserved applause, instantly segued into another...this one an emotionally intense rendition of "My Way."

A woman with large gold earrings and curly silver hair grabbed the microphone from the top of the organ and began filling the club car with the Spanish lyrics of the song. Her husband shouted in encouragement, then lifted a camera to take her picture. The camera's built-in flash filled the club car with portable lightning. The singer reached the second chorus, and the train rolled over the top of the hill and started down.

That was the precise moment Marianne Hanfield first heard what sounded like a series of firecrackers, popping and exploding in a muted burst of noise from the front of the train toward the engine. She was still trying to piece together the exact source of the disturbance when everyone riding in the club car was thrown forward and, with metal wheels screeching upon the narrow-gauge tracks, the train ground to a halt.

Jessica looked at her mother for answers. "Mom?"

"I don't know, honey," the woman replied. "Maybe they're having engine trouble."

"At least we know it's not a flat tire," Ron joked.

The popping noises grew louder, and the lady holding the microphone screamed, pointing a trembling finger in the direction of the road running next to the tracks. A car had swerved in front of the Transcantabrico's bus, stopping it in its path.

"Oh, my God!" Marianne exclaimed in horrified disbelief.

The driver of the bus was rising from his seat when the passenger door of the car blocking his way slammed open, and an angry man with a gun in his hands leaped out. The bus driver lifted his hands in self-defense as the machine gunner opened fire. Marianne recognized the sound at once—the same popping noise she had heard before.

The windshield of the bus caved in, imploding under the relentless barrage of bullets. Glass flew everywhere. The helpless driver seemed to disintegrate, disappearing in a murky splash of red and shadows.

The cold-blooded killer raised his weapon above his head in a jubilant gesture of triumph, then set his sights on new worlds to conquer and ran toward the train.

Frozen by shock, Marianne Hanfield regained her senses as a wave of pandemonium swept the club car from end to end. Pushing herself away from the table with enough force to topple her chair, Marianne heaved to her feet and called her children.

"Jessica! Ron!" the woman yelled, frantically waving her hands and urging them to snap out of the state of stunned immobility that had gripped her. "We have to get out of here. Now!"

But even as her teenage daughter and son raced to obey her command, one of the doors leading into the club car flew open, and a half-dozen cousins of the bus driver's killer rushed inside. The woman who had been singing shrieked into the microphone as one of the first gunmen through the door caught her with a chopping spray of machine gunfire. The microphone went flying, and the woman was blasted off her feet and into the lap of the organist.

Seeing his wife's savage murder, the dead woman's husband cried out in rage and charged at her killer, taking no more than a couple of steps before a stream of lead from another killer's gun cut him to ribbons. He stopped as though hit by an invisible fist, and the built-in flash of the camera he still held flashed twice. His legs buckled beneath him, and he corkscrewed to the floor. The camera bounced from his fist and landed under a chair.

Ron Hanfield was only seventeen, but he was man enough to know his mother and sister were doomed if he failed to protect them. Tugging his stunned sister to her feet, he pulled her around the side of the table and began herding her to the back of the club car.

"The other door!" he shouted to his mother. "It's our only chance!"

Marianne nodded in silence and reached out to take her daughter's arm when the rest of the killers opened random fire on the passengers. The American woman's young son was one of the first to die as the terrorists' attack erupted in a flurry of bullets and death.

Three bullets struck Ron Hanfield in the back, drilling a grisly route through his body and escaping from his chest in a single gaping hole. The boy gasped, threw his hands into the air and relinquished his hold on his sister. He managed a final look into his mother's eyes, then stumbled to his right in a sideways death-dive as he crashed against a table.

"Ronny!" The boy's mother was oblivious to the carnage sweeping the club car as she fell to her knees and cradled her dead son's head in her arms. "Ronny!"

A hand clutched her shoulder, and Marianne looked up, staring through a veil of tears into the frightened face of her daughter. The woman frowned. Try as she might, she couldn't remember the girl's name. Funny about that. She almost laughed.

The interior of the club car was a caldron of death, a shooting gallery whose flesh-and-blood targets were swiftly becoming extinct. The dead and dying were everywhere. Only Marianne and her daughter appeared unaffected by the slaughter.

Someone hollered in Spanish, and the shooting suddenly stopped. Marianne blinked, shaking the ringing din of the gunshots from her ears. What was she to do now? Ronny was dead and . . .

"Mommy!" her daughter cried out, and Marianne struggled to free herself of the deadweight of her son. Cruel hands were digging into her daughter's shoulders, and Marianne moaned aloud when she saw the face of the bus driver's slayer looming over hers.

Without thinking, Marianne lashed out at the man, clawing him across the side of his face and drawing blood as her fingernails raked his skin. She came at him with her other hand, but he was too fast, catching her fist in an iron grip, squeezing and crushing her fingers. The butt of a rifle smacked the woman's head, and she groaned, staggering in reverse in a haze of confusion as she lost her balance and hit the floor.

"Mommy!" the girl whimpered as the laughing killer tore away half of her blouse. "Mommy!"

Feebly Marianne lifted her arms and recalled her daughter's name. "Jessica . . ."

Holding his nubile prize in tow, the girl's attacker withdrew a handgun and grinned at her mother.

Jessica, realizing what was about to happen, struggled to free herself and divert the gunman's aim. "Mommy, don't let him shoot you! Mommy!"

"Hace mucho tiempo que no tengo una pichada," the leering killer informed Marianne, then the gun in his hand came to life with twin claps of thunder.

Two streaks of fire burned their way through Marianne's chest. She wanted to cry out but couldn't. Even her tears had deserted her. Death settled upon her like an unwanted blanket. All she could do was watch helplessly as her Jessica was dragged, kicking and screaming, in the direction of the sleeper cars.

Marianne opened her mouth to speak, but no words came.

1

It rained on the day of the funerals, spilling down in a sticky downpour that drenched the mourners and filled the grave sites with mud. The nation was already numb from seeing its citizens, and those of other lands, fall prey to the whims of terrorists, and the grim aftermath of the Transcantabrico tragedy hit the people of the United States particularly hard.

Altogether, fifteen Americans had perished in the assault on the Spanish train, while the remaining victims of the attack originated from the United Kingdom, the Far East, Germany, Italy and France. Worldwide condemnation for the wanton murder of innocents was virtually unanimous. Even the Soviet Union publicly voiced its outrage at the cowardly act of violence.

Of the fifteen dead Americans, most were in their graves, laid to rest before their time was due. Only the services for Marianne Hanfield and her two children remained to be performed. The sorrow expressed by the Hanfield family's relatives was compounded by the heartfelt tide of emotion sweeping the nation.

Media coverage of the funerals had transformed the occasion into a national day of mourning. Burdened with the uselessness of lives cut short, the nation's collective questions were "Why?" and "Would the killers responsible ever be found?"

One man, standing solemnly at the back of the crowd of mourners, knew the answer to at least one of those questions. Yes, he silently promised himself, the killers *would* be found, and they would be made to pay the ultimate price for their vicious strike against all things decent.

The man's promise was no idle boast. He had the ways and the means to fulfill his vow. The man's name was Hal Brognola and, as director of the ultrasecret Stony Man Farm in the Blue Ridge Mountains of Virginia, he had at his command the international terrorists' worst enemy—the five-man supersquad known as Phoenix Force.

Stony Man Farm, with the blessing of the President of the United States, had originally been created to capitalize on the talents of Mack Bolan, the one and only Executioner. Bolan had come to the end of his relentless war against the Mafia at a time when global terrorism was reaching epidemic proportions. Terrormongers were butchering their victims with impunity, without fear of reprisal from anyone.

Mack Bolan changed all that and, in doing so, enlisted the trusted aid of the finest antiterrorists in the world. A cancer was eating away at humanity's heart, and Bolan knew it would take a special breed of soldier to eradicate the disease without killing the patient. Phoenix Force met the Executioner's stringent criteria for excellence, and exceeded them; they were five who fought like five hundred, fearless soldiers who willingly stormed the hellgrounds of the world again and again so that freedom-loving people of all nationalities could live their lives in peace.

Brognola stuck a beat-up cigar into his mouth. Chewing on it absently, he looked into the distance with a concerned and faraway look in his eyes. As the nation's top federal agent, he had seen enough to turn most hardened men to jelly. Which was not to imply that he didn't have feelings.

Brognola cared, all right. To the depths of his soul, he cared. He had devoted his life to righting wrongs, and was not going to stop now. The victims of the Transcantabrico disaster might have been silenced, but they would never be forgotten—not while he had anything to say about it.

The Transcantabrico killers might think they had committed their crime with impunity, but they were mistaken. Brognola knew this as a certainty. The killers might have escaped for now, but the long arm of retribution would find and destroy them.

The men of Phoenix Force wouldn't have it any other way.

2

It was three cigars demolished and counting, when the five-man supercrew of Phoenix Force entered the war room of Stony Man headquarters.

"Blimey!" David McCarter peered into the ashtray used by the head Fed. "You're like the smokestack of an unused factory. Whatever did those cigars do to you?"

Brognola grinned, shoving the cigar into the corner of his mouth. "I didn't think you'd mind me going through the motions."

"Not mind?" the Cockney complained as he took a seat. "Of course I mind." He slipped a Player's cigarette from the pack in his pocket and promptly started to pollute the war room's air. "I bloody well have to take the blame alone, don't I?"

"While the rest of us try to breathe," Gary Manning protested while he sought out the farthest seat from McCarter he could find. The broad-shouldered Canadian settled into his chair with a sigh. "You're an enigma, McCarter... a walking tobacco leaf."

"Thank you," McCarter said, unperturbed.

Colonel Yakov Katzenelenbogen rounded the conference table and sat next to Brognola, then waited quietly while Calvin James and Rafael Encizo found seats. After everyone had taken their place, the Fed turned to Katz. "Glad to see you up and around, Yakov."

"I'm glad to *see* period," Yakov Katzenelenbogen replied with a smile. "And I'm ready to go back to work."

The unit commander of Phoenix Force had been temporarily blinded by an explosion and had been hospitalized in Arlington, Virginia, until recently. It had been the first time since Phoenix Force had been assembled that Katz hadn't participated in a mission. The other four men had been out of the country on assignment to Kenya while Katz was recuperating. However, Katz hadn't found his hospital stay boring. A romance with a lady doctor and a murder attempt by two young Nazi fanatics had seen to that.

"I don't suppose our being here today has anything to do with what's happened in Spain?" Katz got to the subject at hand.

Brognola nodded. "Every reason in the world, Katz. The turmoil surrounding the brutal attack of the Transcantabrico has triggered an international uproar. One that shows no signs of letting up, even without knowing where to point the finger of blame. There are rumors of a Spanish trade embargo brewing until the matter is dealt with."

"Having sixty people killed for no apparent reason is bound to garner some kind of reaction," Katz concluded. "It's only natural that the countries would exhibit anger over the killing of their citizens. Their people were murdered in Spain and, until they know differently, they no doubt will hold the Spanish government responsible.''

"Which is pretty much how the countries in question are playing their hand," Brognola confirmed. "They've seen their citizens fall prey to mindless violence, and they're demanding justice—or else."

"Again," Katz added, "their reaction is understandable. Without an identifiable party to single out as the one pulling the strings behind the attack, venting all their frustration in Spain's direction is the next best thing. It's not going to solve the mystery of why the Transcantabrico's passengers were killed, but it will serve, albeit temporarily, to keep the public satisfied that something is being done to remedy the situation."

With his slightly paunchy midsection, peaceful blue eyes and iron-gray hair, Yakov Katzenelenbogen could have easily passed for a university professor longing for an early retirement and an abundance of free time. However, the saying "Never judge a book by its cover" was never more true than with the Phoenix team's unit commander.

For close to forty years Katz was the answer to seemingly insurmountable problems, starting in his teens when he joined the French Resistance and battled against Nazi tyranny during World War II, and continuing when he fought alongside the forces of the Haganah to help Israel's bid for independence. Once that goal was met, the man whom Hal Brognola and the rest of Phoenix Force knew as one of the most formidable counterterrorists in the world honed his skills to perfection as a member of Mossad.

If anything about the Israeli's physical appearance hinted at the nature of his chosen profession, it was the fact that his right arm had been amputated just below the elbow—an outcome of his participation in the same Six Day War that had claimed the life of his only son.

"Any takers claiming a prize for the hit yet?" Encizo asked.

Brognola chomped thoughtfully on his cigar. "Some group dubbing itself the Brothers of Allah telephoned a Madrid radio station after news of the massacre was released to the media, but a cursory investigation by the Spanish police determined that the so-called confessors to the crime were a couple of local teenagers looking for a little excitement to enliven an otherwise boring afternoon. The two kids were severely reprimanded by the authorities and then released to the custody of their parents. Obviously, their prank earned them more excitement than they bargained for."

"A lesson," Encizo guessed, "that no doubt began to sink in somewhere in the vicinity of the seat of their pants."

Rafael Encizo had been a member of Phoenix Force since the antiterrorist team's first mission. With communism and Castro working in concert to obliterate all freedom in his native homeland, the Cuban-born soldier had participated in the Bay of Pigs invasion in 1961.

When that ill-fated venture turned sour, Encizo was captured and presented as a gift to the Communist sadists running El Principe—the infamous prison dedicated to making life hell on earth for Castro's political enemies. Enduring a regimen of "behavior-modification techniques" devised by Soviet "technicians" determined to make anyone see Red and like it, the stocky Cuban survived their torturous practices and proved them wrong, breaking his guard's neck one day and making good his escape.

Finding his way back to the U.S. shores, Encizo turned his attention to occupations that enabled him to master a variety of skills. These included work as a scuba instructor, a treasure hunter and a professional bodyguard.

Sometime during the course of events he became a naturalized citizen. When given the nod to join Phoenix Force, Encizo was employed as an insurance investigator specializing in maritime claims.

"So, if the Brothers of Allah turned out to be a dead end," Calvin James said, "then we really don't have any good leads to sink our hooks into."

"Not at this time," Brognola agreed. "No."

James shook his head. "It's damned disgusting. Sixty people chilled for God knows what reason, and the cowardly bastards that offed them are too chickenshit to own up to the deed. You've got it straight from the horse's mouth, Hal. I'm going to enjoy tracking down these miserable cruds. And, guaranteed, when I catch up to them, they're not going to like it one damn bit."

Calvin James, unit medic for Phoenix Force, was a natural survivor whose education in the school of hard knocks began on the streets of Chicago's rough south side. In his neighborhood respect was purchased at the price of quick thinking and fast fists, and James proved early that he possessed both talents.

Instinctively knowing that life had more to offer than the slums of Chicago, James enlisted in the Navy at seventeen and trained as a hospital corpsman. His dedication brought him to the attention of the Navy SEALs program and eventually led to a two-year tour of duty in the jungle hellgrounds of Vietnam.

Wounded during a special-ops mission, he was decorated for valor and honorably discharged. Back stateside, the lanky black's dreams of a new beginning were cut short by personal tragedies that began when his father suffered a fatal heart attack, and culminated with the untimely and violent deaths of his mother and sister.

Studying chemistry and medicine at UCLA courtesy of the GI bill when the multiple tragedies occurred, James switched majors and concentrated on police sciences. Following graduation he signed on with the San Francisco Police Department, and was a member of the SFPD's SWAT team when invited by Phoenix Force to join their ranks.

James readily accepted that invitation and had never looked back.

"What about any privileged information on the Transcantabrico strike, Hal?" Gary Manning asked. "Or are we basically limited to what the public has been told?"

"There's not much more to tell," Brognola said, "with the exception of this." He picked up a white envelope from the table in front of him and opened it. "Evidently, one of the train's passengers was busy taking photographs of his wife at the time of the attack. Both the owner of the camera, as well as the man's spouse, were victims of the assault.''

"But the man succeeded in photographing his assailants before he was killed?'' inquired Manning.

By way of answering, Brognola upended the envelope in his hand and emptied its contents onto the table. The top Fed's actions produced a pair of eight-by-ten glossy photographs. He pushed one picture toward Manning and passed the other one to Katz.

"As you can see," Brognola said as the pictures were examined. "Though both pictures are out of focus and lacking suitable clarity to positively identify the killers, there's still sufficient detail to make out five gunmen framed in the door of the train's club car where many of the slain passengers were found.''

"It's frustrating," Manning said, passing the photo along to James, while Katz handed his picture to Encizo. "The pics show us the killers, but they're still too blurry to get a handle on or to peg a nationality on any of them. It tells us something about who hit the train, but not enough for us to waltz out and nail them.''

Gary Manning was another of Phoenix team's founding members. One of the globe's foremost demolitions experts, the workaholic Canadian was so skilled with explosives that he could practically scramble an egg without breaking its shell.

Serving with the Canadian Armed Forces, Manning spent two years in Vietnam as a special observer attached to the 5th Special Forces. He was one of a handful of his countrymen to be awarded the U.S. Silver Star for valor during the Vietnam conflict.

Then Manning joined the Royal Canadian Mounted Police and was soon transferred to the RCMP's anti-terrorist division. Eventually he was posted in Europe to work alongside West Germany's elite counterterrorist unit, the famed GSG-9.

When the RCMP reevaluated its role in the international espionage game, Manning was recalled to have the newly formed Canadian Security Intelligence Service offer him a desk job and lifetime of indigestion and headaches. He thumbs-downed the job and entered the private sector instead, then married to try to raise a family. That project went belly-up while he and his blushing bride were still opening wedding presents.

Once the divorce was history, Manning was employed as a security consultant for North American International when inducted into Phoenix Force. The team's best sniper, Manning would go to the ends of the earth to combat terrorism in any of its ugly incarnations.

David McCarter accepted one of the glossy photos from Encizo and remarked, "I've seen better, but I've also seen worse. The important thing is that we have an idea now what some of the terrorists look like. That's more than they can say about us. Up to now the killers probably believe they got away." He indicated the photo in his hand. "This picture represents carelessness on their part, and it's going to cost them dearly. If they were careless once, it will happen again.

"Sloppiness has a nasty habit of repeating itself. Leaving the camera behind would have been all right if they had exposed the film inside. The fact that the camera was overlooked says something important about the killers: they're not such clever boys.''

A product of London's colorful and tough East End, David McCarter's background, which brought him to Phoenix Force, was unmatched for its diversity. A veteran of Great Britain's Special Air Service, the fox-faced Englishman saw action in Hong Kong, Oman and Northern Ireland and helped lead the SAS assault on the Iranian embassy in London.

Formerly a national champion of the British Pistol Marksmanship Team, and a master of virtually every form of combat, McCarter was also a superbly trained pilot. Bold, brash, short-tempered and, by some accounts—Manning's in particular—slightly mad at times, McCarter had dedicated his life to fighting the oppressors of freedom everywhere.

''So,'' McCarter continued as he passed the photo back down the line to Brognola, ''when do we leave for Spain?''

Before he could reply, the telephone beside the head Fed began to ring. Answering the call on the second ring, Brognola listened intently for less than thirty seconds, then respectfully thanked the party for calling and hung up.

''That was the President,'' Brognola announced in a somber tone. ''Apparently, the terrorists have struck again.''

''Where this time?'' Katz wanted to know.

''At one of the museums in Madrid,'' Brognola responded. ''Pretty much the same scenario as with the train, only this time the tourists were hit with grenades as well as guns. No exact total on the number of casualties yet, but they're expected to be high. Initial figures suggest as many as twenty-four dead.''

"We can't wait any longer, then," Manning said. "How do we get to Spain?"

"I've arranged for a special flight that will take you directly into Torrejon Air Force Base, fifteen miles northeast of Madrid. The base commander at Torrejon has orders to let you bring any kind of equipment you think you may need."

"That'll take care of our weaponry requirements," Katz said. "What about the Spanish authorities? What's our angle with them?"

"As far as the Spanish police are concerned, you five are part of an American investigative team sent to Spain in connection with the Transcantabrico massacre. Don't expect them to greet you with open arms, though," Brognola said. "Far from it. They've agreed to let you operate in Spain, but only reluctantly, and only after Washington pressured the Spanish government to give the green light for international cooperation in the investigation. Spain's letting you in, but on the strict precondition that no unnecessary waves are made while you're there."

McCarter stood and shrugged. "Bit out of luck on that one, mate."

3

Ruben Saldana wasn't a fast runner, a fact that often made him late for work. An assistant to an assistant of the director of the Spanish delegation to the European Economic Community headquarters in Brussels, Saldana dreaded each morning with a passion seconded only to his dislike for Belgian television programs.

Saldana's discomfort had everything to do with Belgian motorists' attitude toward pedestrians, who were not regarded as people trying to cross the street but as slowly moving targets created to annoy impatient drivers. That was why Saldana hated going to work.

Anyone in Brussels—and Saldana had solicited plenty of opinions on the subject—would have agreed that the last place in the city where pedestrians could feel safe was the notorious Rond Point Schuman traffic circle. Nor were these opinions the product of idle speculation: a cursory examination of death toll statistics proved that.

As something less than a world-class sprinter, Saldana knew he should avoid the Rond Point Schuman traffic circle at all costs. But the building where he worked fronted that very same traffic circle, and Saldana had no choice but to put his life on the line crossing the Rond Point Schuman twice a day, ten times a week.

Attributing his miraculous survival record to date to the combination of fervent prayer and shoes with traction, Saldana was counting the days until the end of his twelve-month assignment in Brussels. To Saldana's way of thinking, his return to sunny Spain couldn't happen soon enough.

Standing at the edge of the curb, Saldana watched the Belgian motorists race by. Across the traffic circle, beyond the stream of speeding automobiles, the EEC building was in plain sight.

Absently Saldana checked the dial on his watch. He had ten minutes. With luck he could cross with the next break in traffic and be sitting behind his desk and at work on time for a change. Unfortunately, he noted warily, glancing from side to side, more than two dozen other pedestrians gathered around him had the same idea.

All at once the mood of the pedestrians surrounding Saldana shifted into high gear. People stopped talking and concentrated instead on more important matters. A traffic break was coming. The crowd sensed it. So did he.

Then it was there, a wide-open inviting space, stretching from the curb clear to the opposite side of the traffic circle. Saldana swallowed. It was now or never. The crowd surged forward, and Saldana's right foot left the curb.

He hesitated, wondering if the traffic break would last long enough for him to make it across. His briefcase was an anchor attached to his fist. Could he run carrying such a heavy load? Impossible. He put his right foot back on the curb, and the break in the flow of Brussels' morning traffic mended itself.

Alone at the curb and cursing his moment of weakness, Saldana stared forlornly at the EEC building. He was going to be late again. His only other hope would be for a British car to approach the traffic circle. Drivers from England were known for courtesy, and were the only ones likely to stop.

Five minutes later, though, Saldana was on the verge of seeking out the nearest public telephone and calling for a taxicab when a four-door sedan entered Rond Point Schuman traffic circle and began to brake immediately.

Saldana was perplexed and suspicious. What new game was that? The approaching sedan slowed even more, and Saldana's confusion increased when the driver of the vehicle—decidedly Spanish in appearance, now that Saldana could see him better—pulled the car to the edge of the curb next to where he stood.

A man riding in the back seat rolled down his window and leaned out, addressing Saldana by name.

"Yes?" Saldana said, smiling and stepping forward.

The car's rear door swung open, and the man in the back trained a gun at Saldana. "Get in."

4

"Welcome to Torrejon," James announced as their USAF C-141B completed its final approach to the runway below. Home to the units of the Sixteenth Air Force and the 401st Tactical Fighter Wing, Torrejon Air Force Base ranked number three among the busiest military airports in Europe.

The wheels of the aircraft touched down, and McCarter was the first to unbuckle his seat belt. "Last one off is a rotten egg."

"Don't get in my way, then," Katz warned, chewing the last of his antacid tablets to calm his flight-weary stomach. "Was it my imagination or did our ride over here seem excessively bumpy?"

"I didn't notice any turbulence," McCarter said.

"How could you?" Manning asked. "You were asleep most of the way."

"Just resting my eyes," McCarter shot back.

The jet slowed and followed a taxiway that took the C-141B away from Torrejon's main passenger terminal and toward a large hangar that was conspicuously devoid of any external activity. The remaining members of Phoenix Force undid their seat belts as the aircraft finally came to a stop and its engines shut down. Katz stood and led the way from the plane, with the rest of the team close behind.

"Mr. Feldman?"

"Yes." Katz acknowledged his cover name and extended his left hand as he stepped into the hangar. "I'm Feldman."

"Colonel Wagoner. Base commander." Torrejon's senior officer gripped the Israeli's hand in a firm handshake while the other four Stony Man soldiers disembarked.

"My orders," Wagoner continued, "are to assist you and your men with whatever you need during your stay in Spain."

"Thank you, Colonel," Katz said. "All we require at the moment is a vehicle large enough for us and our gear—one that we can have access to on a twenty-four-hour basis."

"I'll have your vehicle available within ten minutes," Wagoner promised, glancing past Manning. "There's just the five of you, then?"

"That's correct," Katz said. "Does that create some kind of problem, Colonel Wagoner?"

"Not at all," the base commander answered. "It's just that I was led to believe Washington was sending in a special task force to deal directly with the recent rash of terrorist attacks Spain experienced. No offense, Mr. Feldman, but this business with the tourists being killed is a whole lot bigger than anyone back in the States imagines. All of Spain is feeling the strain of this mess. Quite honestly, sir, I don't know if the five of you are up to handling it."

"You're right about one thing, Colonel," Katz said.

"What's that?"

"You *don't* know," Katz told him. "Now, about our transportation?"

"Yes, sir. Right away. In the meantime, I'll have to ask all of you to follow me to a building located just in back of this hangar where a representative of the Cuerpo General de Policía is waiting to speak to you."

"Very well," Katz said, aware that the Cuerpo General de Policía was Spain's plainclothes police team, responsible for all criminal investigations in the cities, as well as the more serious crimes committed in country areas. "Show us the way."

Wagoner did, and sixty seconds later Phoenix Force was ushered into an air-conditioned room featuring low overhead lighting and a noticeable absence of windows. A long narrow conference table was positioned in the middle of the room, around which had been placed a dozen high-backed metal chairs with dark green plastic seats.

As they followed Colonel Wagoner into the room, a man who had been leaning against the table quickly came to attention. Wearing an immaculately tailored beige summer suit and a dark brown shirt with a pale yellow tie, the man looked to be in his mid-thirties.

He had wavy black hair that was shellacked into place, a ruggedly handsome face and on his left hand a diamond ring big enough to hock for a small fortune. Altogether, he could have passed for someone who had just stepped from the pages of a fashion magazine.

McCarter wanted to laugh.

"Mr. Feldman," Wagoner spoke, "this is Lieutenant Colonel Diaz, the *comisario* of the Cuerpo General de Policía. *Comisario*...Mr. Feldman."

The Israeli and the Spaniard shook hands as Colonel Wagoner excused himself to make arrangements for Phoenix Force's transportation needs. Katz broke the handshake and introduced each of his men by their cover names.

"Gentlemen," Diaz began, speaking in fluid but accented English after the formalities of the introductions were out of the way. "Let me first welcome you to Spain and express my sincere grief for the tragic incidents that have brought you to my country. Such senseless violence is never easy to accept, and even less so when so many innocent lives have been affected one way or another—either the unfortunate victims themselves, or the families they have left behind. Everyone in Spain, without exception, is outraged by these terrorist acts.

"That said, let me formally state it is the Cuerpo General de Policía's position that your intrusion into my department's ongoing investigation of these crimes is greatly discouraged. While it is true that, proportionately, American citizens have comprised the greater number of victims lost in both attacks, each of the crimes was committed on Spanish soil. Our jurisdiction. Not yours.

"We did not invite you here. We do not want you here. And we openly confess to having no need at all for whatever services you feel capable of rendering. In short, I must ask you to reconsider your proposed mission in my country, and respectfully request that you abandon it and secure arrangements to return to the United States at your earliest convenience.''

"A request," Katz informed Diaz, "that, I am afraid, we must 'respectfully' ignore. My men and I are staying."

"Very well, Señor Feldman," Diaz said. "I trust you will not personally take what I have just told you to heart."

"Of course not," Katz said. "I understand how you and your fellow officers must feel, but please believe that our goal in seeking out the culprits responsible for these terrible murders is the same as yours. We don't ask that you like the fact that we're here, but would hope that we could be permitted to go about our business with a minimum of interference."

"And what precisely is your business, Señor Feldman?"

Katz fished his Camels from his shirt pocket and offered one to Diaz. Katz lit both smokes with a disposable lighter, then answered, "We have been sent to Spain to conduct an independent investigation into the terrorist attacks, compile any information we deem pertinent to the case, and then to act accordingly on the basis of what we have learned."

Diaz frowned. "What do you mean? To what extent are you and your men prepared to go?"

"Whatever it takes to ensure that the terrorists you and I are both looking for are stopped for good," Katz said. "We all want the same thing. If you find the terrorists first, fine. I am sure you will know what to do with them. If we find them first, we shall know, too."

"Very well, Señor Feldman," Diaz sighed, "I can see that my plea for you and your associates to leave Spain is wasted, so I will now inform you about developments that transpired while you and your men were still in the air. I have nothing to gain by keeping this information secret since media coverage of what I reveal is a certainty by late this afternoon."

"We appreciate any information you can supply," Katz said. "Now, what is it you have to tell us?"

"This morning in Belgium," Diaz said, "a minor official assigned to the Spanish offices of the Common Market's headquarters in Brussels was discovered murdered—executed with a shot to the back of the head, his body unceremoniously dumped from a moving automobile in front of the building where he worked."

"How does his death tie in with the tourist killings here?" Encizo asked.

"Pinned to the dead man's clothes was a note," Diaz replied, "a note claiming responsibility for the strike against the Transcantabrico and, more recently, the grenade and gun attack at the museum in Madrid. It stated that the number of tourists killed up to now represents only the tip of a very bloody iceberg unless Spain immediately withdraws from the EEC."

"Diabolical," McCarter muttered under his breath.

"Until my government openly initiates steps to secure Spain's departure from the European Economic Community," Diaz went on, "any and all tourists visiting Spain will be considered fair game for future terrorist attacks."

"Was the note signed?" James asked.

Diaz nodded. "By a group calling itself the Iberian League."

"Never heard of them," Manning said.

"Neither has anyone else," Diaz confessed. "Yet, until we know otherwise, we must assume that this Iberian League exists."

"I agree," Katzenelenbogen said. "The contents of the note must be taken seriously, especially since so much trouble was taken to deliver the note in Brussels. Pinning the note to a dead man makes for one hell of a calling card."

"No lie," James commented, "plus it tells us how wacko these Iberian League dudes really are." He nodded to Diaz. "What was your government's reaction to the Iberian League's demands?"

"What else can it be?" Diaz returned. "My government has no intention to withdraw from the Common Market. For them to pretend otherwise would stretch credibility to the point of breaking. Who would believe it? Deep down I do not even think the mysterious Iberian League would accept such nonsense.

"After nearly four hundred years, Spain has come out of its isolationist shell and joined hands with its European neighbors. It is ridiculous to suggest that such progress, such an important step forward for the nation is to suddenly and irrevocably be brought to a halt because some terrorist group does not wish Spain to become part of the twentieth century.

"My government worked long and hard to overcome the pariah mentality associated with Spain under the Franco regime, but we have succeeded. Spain has gained entry into the EEC and will never abandon such a major accomplishment.''

"Meanwhile," McCarter offered, "until the Iberian League yobbos are dealt with, more innocent people will be killed."

"I am afraid so," Diaz said. "Which is why the people behind the Iberian League must be found. Time is of the essence here. The terrorists' note said it all: they have declared open season on Spain's tourists."

"Yes," Katz concurred. "Well, perhaps my friends and I will soon have the opportunity to do a little hunting of our own."

"I am not positive I like the implication of your statement, Señor Feldman," Diaz said. "Where do you propose this hunt of yours begin?"

Katz finished his smoke and ground out the butt in an ashtray on the table. "Madrid."

5

The men in the first four rows of the otherwise deserted theater sat conversing among themselves, comparing notes and sharing observations, reliving the exciting events of the past few days over and over again, while waiting for the ceremony to begin. With each retelling, the details behind the Transcantabrico attack and the assault on the crowded museum grew in scope until the twin strikes became the greatest Spanish event since General Franco's timely death.

Three lecterns were placed side by side on the theater's bare stage, each of the wooden podiums bathed in a pool of cool blue light. The faded curtains were drawn apart and attached with thick golden sashes to the sides of the proscenium arch, while the grand drape sagging above the act curtain threatened to collapse at any second.

A prerecorded drumroll sounded through the theater's antiquated public address system. A hush fell over the crowd. The taped introduction ran its course, and the three men whom the others had come to hear made their entrance onto the stage. The audience applauded enthusiastically as each of the men appeared.

Moving first to the lectern placed downstage right was the Spanish shipbuilding magnate, Fernando Campos. In his fifties, tall, silver haired and with an angular jawline that jutted from his face like the prow of a ship, Campos exuded the full confidence of a man in control of his environment.

Next out of the chute was José Mantanez. A year younger than Campos, and standing six inches shorter, Mantanez was a successful financier whose substantial holdings in Spain's olive oil and domestic wine industries easily qualified him as one of his country's wealthiest citizens.

Mantanez had lost most of his hair through hereditary baldness, but he carried close to thirty pounds of excess baggage around his waist. He negotiated a turn as soon as he came on stage and stepped in back of the lectern downstage left.

Last to appear, yet doing so to the clamor of continued applause from the audience, was Eduardo Vera. The eldest of his colleagues at sixty-seven, he approached the center-stage podium with a noticeable limp. Vera held the controlling interest in Spain's second-largest steel manufacturing firm.

Immaculately dressed and sporting a white carnation in the lapel of his suit coat, Vera allowed the applause to go on for another few seconds, then raised the index finger of his right hand for the audience to quiet. A moment later he had his wish, and glanced first to Campos, then across to Mantanez, before electing to speak.

"Good afternoon, my friends," Vera began. "On behalf of my illustrious associates and myself, I want to welcome you today to this most important celebration in which we come together to commemorate the recent victories of our beloved Iberian League."

Vera paused for applause and was not disappointed.

"I have heard it said," Vera continued, "that the true Spanish patriot questions not the actions or policies of his elected officials. The true Spanish patriot, I have heard, blindly follows wherever his elected officials may lead.

"If that is so, my friends, then I humbly submit to you that I am not a Spanish patriot. If that is so, my brothers, then I humbly submit to you that I am a traitor to my own people.

"Yes." Vera's voice rose above the applause that greeted his confession. "It is true. If a Spanish patriot is only what they say, then I *am* a traitor!"

Vera turned with a flourish of his arms to his right. "Señor Campos *is* a traitor!" he shouted, then twisted to his left. "Señor Mantanez *is* a traitor! And, yes, my brothers...*all* of you are traitors, too!"

Vera made his last statement with his arms outstretched to the crowd as though he had watched a film on the life of Mussolini the night before. The audience's response was a boisterous combination of hand clapping, foot stomping, whistles and yells. They were being worked into a frenzy of passion for their cause, and they were loving every minute. Vera gave them room to run with their exuberance, then carried on.

"Spain's greatest natural resource has always been the Spanish people. Our strength as a nation has always come from within. But now, the value of that most sacred of resources has been cast aside. Now that strength has been contaminated and diluted by the waters of foreign influence.

"Our leaders would have the world believe that all of Spain rejoiced when, after fierce negotiations, the European Economic Community at last opened its doors to Spain. Our leaders would have the world believe that Spain's entry into the Common Market heralded the dawn of a new age of prosperity.

"But prosperity for whom? For Spanish farmers who must adapt to standards set by foreigners so that they can enjoy the dubious honor of competing with the inferior agricultural products of Italy, England, West Germany and France? Already we are seeing the result of such disastrous competition with the failure of many of our smaller family farms, northwest of us in Galicia. Is that how our leaders reward hard work and dedication? Where is the honor in stealing a man's right to provide for his family?"

"There is no honor!" one of Eduardo Vera's more fervent listeners proclaimed. "To steal a man's livelihood is a sin!"

"A sin, indeed," Vera readily agreed. "And yet Spanish farms continue to fail, cheap Italian wines flood our domestic market, and Spain's steel and shipbuilding industries are being forced into the corner of financial extinction. The import duty our competitors have had to pay on their goods, often as high as forty percent, is being phased out; in five years' time the duty will be history. And after that, what?

Will the pride and productivity of the Spanish people be history, too?''

''No!'' came the thunderous response to Vera's question.

''Make no mistake, my brothers,'' Vera said. ''There are those who *will* prosper from our nation's unfortunate entry into the Common Market, but those who benefit will not have a single drop of Spanish blood in their veins. Those who prosper will be foreign vultures intent on devouring the body of our Spain until only a carcass remains.

''But we, the Iberian League, say no to the vultures. And so long as our leaders blindly steer us down the path of doom, we will dedicate our very lives to turning away the foreign oppressors and giving Spain back to the Spanish!''

The cheering crowd rose to its feet, drowning out Vera's words, forcing him to wait a full minute and a half before he could finish his speech.

''Spain's leaders may have given up on Spain, but not us,'' the eloquent Vera announced. ''Spain's true patriots have not abandoned the nation to European vultures. Spain's true patriots will reverse the treacherous course our leaders have set us on. We are Spain's one hope for salvation. The Iberian League. Today, tomorrow . . . forever!''

And with that Eduardo Vera produced a silk handkerchief from his coat and unashamedly wiped away the tears misting his eyes. Mantanez and Campos, succumbing to the stirring emotional content of Vera's words, did the same. Finally, after a suitable demonstration for the audience that the three businessmen were among the Iberian League's most ardent supporters, Fernando Campos urged the audience members to sit, and then addressed them for the very first time.

"As Señor Vera has told you," Campos said, "we have come together this afternoon to commemorate our Iberian League's success in graphically displaying to our leaders that, until they are willing to withdraw from the EEC, no foreign tourists visiting Spain will be safe. It is regrettable, I know, that such drastic measures had to be taken, but our leaders left us no alternative.

"To save Spain, innocents must die. Yet their deaths, however sad, are a small price to pay to force our leaders to realize that not all Spanish patriots are content to see our nation plundered and destroyed.

"You men should be proud. You have done well. Your devastating efficiency aboard the Transcantabrico excursion train, your work yesterday at the Prado gallery, and again this morning with your triumph in Brussels . . . all of you are to be congratulated. Señor Campos, Señor Mantanez and I salute you. But mere congratulations are not enough to express our gratitude for a job well done. It is our view that exceptional work deserves more than a smile and a handshake.

"Such praise might make you feel good, but it doesn't do anything to impress the balance of your bank account. For that reason, my esteemed associates and myself have elected to issue bonus payments of ten thousand pesetas to every Iberian League member who participated in the aforementioned strikes.''

Campos held up his hand to still the cries of approval rising from the crowd. "And for those of you who haven't yet had the opportunity to qualify for such bonuses, do not despair. Our nation's leaders are a stubborn lot, and there are sure to be many more chances for you to share in the many rewards our united brotherhood has to offer. Rest assured, you have my word, my brothers. You will never see the day when the Iberian League forgets you as our leaders have forgotten Spain.''

The audience was still engaged in reacting to what Campos had told them when José Mantanez, having patiently waited for his turn to speak, jumped in with his contribution to the day's activities.

"Before we close our meeting by handing out the bonus payments," Mantanez said, his bald scalp reflecting the bluish glow of the spotlight overhead, "we have one final piece of important business to attend to. In any venture with overwhelming odds, it is inevitable that certain individuals, distinguished by their actions in the field, make it necessary for those at the top of the chain of command to sit up and take notice.

"To that end—" Mantanez paused, noisily clearing his throat "—I would like to ask Roberto Conejo to join me here on stage. Roberto Conejo?" He squinted into the spotlight hitting him in the eyes. "Are you out there?"

Conejo *was* out there and, in an instant, he was on his feet and running up the aisle toward the steps leading to the stage. His face a mask of greedy excitement, Conejo climbed the steps and crossed at once to where José Mantanez was waiting.

"Those of you not participating in the Transcantabrico assault," Mantanez said once Conejo was in place, "missed the rare opportunity of seeing this man in action."

Conejo's chest swelled with pride.

"The orders for the attack on the train were simple," Mantanez explained. "Our men were to bring the train to a halt, enter the train, and then dispose of the train's passengers and crew in an orderly manner. By and large, those simple directions were followed to the letter...with the sole exception of Roberto Conejo."

Conejo shifted his weight from one foot to the other and grinned uneasily.

"With little experience at following such basic instructions, however," Mantanez said, "Roberto Conejo, the man standing next to me and before you now, decided to bend the rules to suit his own tastes. Yes, it is true Roberto was willing to dispose of the train's passengers, but in the case of his final victim, a fourteen-year-old girl from the United States, Roberto decided to save ammunition in favor of raping the child, and then strangling her.

"Granted, as leaders of your Iberian League, we could have overlooked Roberto's transgression, but at what cost? Unless all of us understand right from the start that the rules and regulations we set down are not meant to be broken, then utter chaos is sure to result. Roberto Conejo did not follow the rules. Raping and strangling a fourteen-year-old girl was not what he was told to do.

"We of the Iberian League are not animals, yet Roberto Conejo's behavior would suggest otherwise. That is because, my brothers, Roberto Conejo prefers to act like an animal instead of acting like a man. So be it. That is his choice. His privilege. But it is also our choice and option to exclude such beasts from our ranks.

"Animals have their place in the scheme of things, and that place is not as a member of the Iberian League. Roberto Conejo behaved like an animal, so it is as an animal he shall be treated." Mantanez turned to Conejo. "Is there anything you could possibly offer in defense of your reprehensible actions?"

Conejo shrugged, dumbfounded, staring in open-mouthed wonder at Mantanez as he searched for something to say and came up blank. When first called to appear on the stage, he had entertained visions of a special bonus above and beyond the first one the rest of his assault team were getting. Now, to be publicly humiliated before his peers instead was more of a blow to his ego than he could begin to contemplate without having his knees start knocking together.

"Well?" Mantanez prodded.

"No." Conejo lowered his chin to his chest, barely speaking above a whisper. "There is no defending my actions, Señor Mantanez. I attacked the girl, raped her and then choked the life out of her body…just as you said. I did the deed, so there is no use denying it. I admit it was wrong. I am sorry."

Mantanez sighed with complete understanding and pulled a small revolver from inside his coat. "So am I."

Conejo's eyes went wide as Mantanez fired the gun at nearly point-blank range, the single bullet crashing through the side of Conejo's skull in a sudden burst of blood. Conejo raised his hands to cover the wound, but died before his fingers could complete the move. His shoulders slumped, his knees caved in, and he flopped to the hardwood surface of the stage with a thump that was heard even above the reverberating report of the gun. Conejo danced in place as life drained from his body, then stopped altogether when whatever song he was listening to came to an end.

José Mantanez reholstered his handgun, then calmly told his shocked audience, "Today, my brothers, you have learned a valuable lesson. Remember it well," he said, pointing to the body at his feet, "and mourn not this animal's passing. Better to take this lesson to heart so that it need not be repeated. Do I make myself clear?"

The resounding *yes* that came in response to his question could have been heard as far north as the Pyrenees.

"Very good, then," Mantanez said. "We shall consider the lesson learned. Now, unless there is anything else for us to..."

Mantanez stopped midsentence as one of the Iberian League's junior officers entered the stage from the wings off left and crossed immediately to the center-stage podium and Eduardo Vera. The newcomer conversed confidentially with Vera, who listened for half a minute before turning with a look of grim determination on his face to inform the audience of the junior officer's news.

"My brothers," Vera said, "I have just been informed of a matter of great importance to our Iberian League. It has been confirmed that the United States has sent a party of investigators to Spain to learn more about our recent activities. It is our desire," he spoke for Mantanez and Campos, "that they learn nothing that will bring them closer to us. I do not yet have the information available as to where these investigators will be staying, but when that information does become known, I want the Americans eliminated. The task of doing so should enable those of you who missed out on the earlier strikes to get your feet wet, plus it will serve to put you in line to receive the same kind of bonus the others are due to be paid.

"Apparently, only five Americans have been sent to Madrid, which means I want at least twelve of you to deal with them when the time comes. Who would like to volunteer?"

Each soldier in the Iberian League raised his hand into the air, calling out that he was ready to send the American meddlers to their graves. In the end Vera was generous in his selection and handpicked fifteen men for the job.

6

"Is it all right to unclench my fingers?" Manning asked. "My knuckles are starting to get sore."

"Shut your gob," McCarter said, deliberately whipping their van in and out of Madrid's congested traffic with the kind of wild abandon Manning detested. "Nothing wrong with my driving, mate."

"Nothing a driver's education course couldn't cure," agreed the Canadian. "How on earth the likes of you ever managed to get behind a wheel and qualify for a driver's license is beyond me."

McCarter laughed. "Who said I had a flaming license?"

Because of the time of their departure from Torrejon air base, Phoenix Force was entering Spain's capital city during the third of Madrid's four daily rush hours. Even so, McCarter seemed not to notice, substituting whatever anxiety the local Madrileños might have felt for traveling through the late afternoon congestion in favor of his Cockney-bred optimism that they would have no difficulty reaching their hotel safely and in one piece. If Gary Manning even remotely shared McCarter's optimism, however, he kept such feelings to himself.

Heading for the almond-shaped central part of the city, they found it impossible not to notice the virtual lack of single-unit houses. Instead, apartment buildings dominated the area. On the sidewalks, James noted as they drove, Madrid's pedestrians appeared to be experiencing a rush hour of their own, including mothers with small armies of children in tow, businessmen and women scurrying to and from the city's metro subway system, street corner musicians, shopkeepers and pensioners.

McCarter followed a long line of cars around a corner and soon took their van past the National Palace on their left. One of Madrid's best-known sights, the palace was completed in 1764, and had provided a home for Spain's monarchs for nearly two hundred years. No monarch had occupied it since 1931, and it was primarily a museum housing a multitude of Spain's artifacts under one roof.

To the right of the van Phoenix Force rode in, and directly across from the National Palace, was the Plaza de Oriente, a spacious parklike area replete with formal gardens of well-manicured hedges and fez-shaped trees, a circular fountain and large stone statues of Spanish kings and warriors. Framed against the background of the Plaza de Oriente was the outline of Madrid's famous opera house, the Teatro Real.

Minutes later McCarter brought their van to a not-so-gentle stop before the main entrance to the Hotel Plaza. Usually with the passing of the busy summer tourist season, booking suites at the hotel in October would be relatively easy. To make certain that accommodations would be waiting for them, though, Hal

Brognola had reserved a pair of adjoining suites in advance; one under Katz's cover name of Feldman, the other reserved under McCarter's cover identity, which was Edmonds.

"All ashore who's going ashore," McCarter announced as they reached their destination, an amused expression appearing on the Briton's foxlike features as Manning was the first to exit the van.

Encizo, James and Katz followed next, removing their gear from the van as they did so. A parking attendant approached McCarter's side of the vehicle to deliver the van to the hotel's underground parking complex, but Encizo intervened with a five-hundred-peseta tip and explained to the young man that McCarter would park the van.

The attendant smiled and pocketed Encizo's money, then supplied verbal instructions regarding the best place to secure an empty space in the underground car park.

The Cuban thanked the attendant, then relayed the information to McCarter as he climbed in the front seat of the van next to the Londoner. They delivered the van to the parking lot below the hotel and returned shortly afterward to where the others were waiting.

"All set?" Manning asked, referring to the special alarm system he had installed on the van following their departure from Torrejon air base.

"Set and ready to go," Encizo confirmed. "If anyone messes with the van, we'll be the first to know."

Five minutes later they were officially checked in and upstairs in the suite registered to Katz. While they set about unpacking their bags, they discussed the specifics surrounding their mission to Spain.

"So," Manning said, crossing to the doors leading to the suite's balcony, beyond which Madrid's impressive skyline could be seen stretching southeast of the hotel. "Where do you guys want to start?"

"How about at a restaurant?" suggested James. "I'm starved."

"Be serious," Manning said.

"I am," James replied, then recited, "Everybody knows 'if the fuel don't flow... then the engine don't go.' To really answer your question, though, do any of you think it's worth us taking a look around the vicinity of the Prado?"

"Possibly," Katzenelenbogen said, "but I sincerely doubt it. Whoever these Iberian League characters are, it's my guess they're not likely to return to the scene of the crime. Not when there are so many other potential targets waiting to be exploited. By now they've probably put yesterday's attack on the museum behind them and are hatching plans for their next hit."

"Which should come soon," Encizo said, "because, so far as they're concerned, they're on a roll. Which doesn't automatically mean their next performance has to take place somewhere here in Madrid. In fact, I don't think it will. Look at their strike against the Transcantabrico. That nasty piece of business got off the ground in the middle of nowhere."

"Rafael's right," McCarter added. "These Iberian League sods are going for major impact in order to get their crazy message across, and to do that they're going to want to make it seem like there's no place in Spain that's safe for tourists to visit. They'll be generous with their terror, spread it around.

"No, Madrid might have clues hanging about to steer us in the right direction, but unless they're ginormous clues, the Iberian League is bound to stay a jump or two ahead of us for just a bit more."

Katz nodded. "My feeling exactly. Even if they're using Madrid as home base, their next strike will most likely be launched in another part of Spain. The trick comes in finding out where."

"Yeah," McCarter said, getting up from the chair he was sitting in and going to the suite's telephone, "that's the hard part, all right. I'm going to call down and have a six-pack of Coke sent up with a small bucket of ice."

A knock sounded on the door to the suite, and Encizo called out, *"¿Quién es?"*

"Room service," came the reply in Spanish.

"Un momento," Encizo said.

"Room service?" James repeated. "That was fast."

"Too fast," McCarter agreed suspiciously, glancing at the suite's unused telephone and withdrawing his Browning 9 mm Hi-Power from shoulder leather. "Let's see who's come calling."

Encizo, who had extracted his H&K MP-5 machine pistol from his suitcase, backed away from the door and invited the person standing outside the suite to enter. *"¡Adelante!"*

That was when a small bomb blast blew the door from its hinges, flinging it into the suite and filling the room with a thunderous ball of angry noise. Thrown from his feet by the force of the explosion, Encizo was still sailing to the suite's carpeted floor when four gunmen looking for blood stormed through the wrecked doorway.

The first killer got his wish the hard way, thanks to a pair of Hi-Power man-stoppers McCarter sent his way. Both slugs ripped into the gunman's exposed chest, carving a path through flesh and bone. The gunman stopped, blinked in surprise at the twin fountains spouting from his chest, then folded into a boneless dive to the floor.

The second Iberian League assassin, charging into the suite with equal finesse, was eliminated by Manning, his Eagle .357 Magnum booming to life with a roar that the target never heard. Manning's deadly accuracy had transformed the side of the man's skull into a jagged window exposing brain matter. The killer toppled lifeless to the carpet.

Bullets raked a path toward Encizo as the Havana hotshot recovered from his fall and brought the destructive power of his MP-5 into play, instinctively homing in on the Iberian Leaguer trying to mow him down, stitching the killer from sternum to crotch with a flurry of H&K lead.

Like a string of bloody pearls, a row of holes appeared on the gunman's body. He coughed and showed a stupid grin of pinkish teeth. Then his submachine gun slipped from his grasp, and so did he from life.

Wishing he had been less anxious to become one of the first of his brothers to slay the American investigators, the fourth and last gunman discovered too late that polishing off his enemies was no easy task. This fact of life and death dawned on the killer's diminishing powers of comprehension after McCarter and Manning caught him in a cross fire from which escape was impossible. Hit from two sides at once, the gunman's body jerked from left to right, deciding where it wanted to die. The decision became moot less than a heartbeat later when a volley of shots from Encizo's H&K tossed the killer flat on his back for his remaining life.

The wrecked door had barely found a resting place and was still spraying the air with sawdust and splinters when Katz and James, confident their Stony Man teammates would cope with the initial rush of Iberian League invaders, turned their attention to protecting their flank. Fully aware their adjoining suite could enable additional enemy gunmen to attack from another direction, the Israeli and the American reacted to the potential threat in concert.

His 9 mm Uzi clutched in his left hand, Katz led the way into the suite next door, and James followed the Israeli's example. Behind them, McCarter and the others were tying up the loose ends, while the faintly lit interior of the suite they were in was deserted.

But not for long.

With no pretense of trying to be quiet about it, the door to the suite was kicked open. Four more IL thugs poured into the room, all of them armed with SMGs, the noise of the fighting pulling them forward like a line of iron nails drawn by a magnet. The first of the newcomers motioned for the others to follow and was halfway across the suite before he glimpsed Katz and James concealed in the shadowy twilight of the room.

The killer gasped and shouted a warning, swinging his subgun around to take out the Phoenix Force duo. James got there first with a double dose of heart-break from his Colt Commander that transformed the gunman's cry of alarm into a death-defying scream.

Death won hands down.

Caught by surprise, and unable to backtrack in time to prevent it, two of the Iberian League killers began their mutual ride into premature graves by tripping over the body of the man James had pegged. With their arms flailing helplessly, and swearing in Spanish, the off-balance pair hit the floor.

The last man down clumsily attempted to climb to his feet as Katz's Uzi delivered a fast call to death with a 5-round burst of 9 mm parabellum slugs. The Israeli's action made the latest Iberian League casualty collapse on the man beneath him, who was unaware that he was weighted down with a corpse. The gunman on the floor did his best to shrug himself free, while simultaneously rolling onto his side so he could fire his subgun.

The killer's trigger finger tightened, and hot lead swarmed against the wall where Katz and James stood. By then, the killer saw too late, the wily duo had moved somewhere else. Not that it mattered much to the IL gunman, because Katz corrected his aim and resumed pumping lead.

While Katz concentrated on eliminating the pair sprawled on the floor, Calvin James was kept busy dealing with the last of the gunmen. James fired once with a shot that went high, then was forced to leap behind the doubtful protection of a long sofa just as his opponent's Star Model Z-62 submachine gun chattered to life.

Instantly the bullets began eating a path along the rear of the couch, slightly above where James was getting on intimate terms with the suite's carpeting. The deadly sweep of enemy lead soon reached the end of the sofa and started back in the opposite direction, this time on a course nearly five inches lower, and impossible for James to avoid.

Seeing the writing on the wall, James grasped his Colt in a two-handed grip and suddenly popped into view, catching the Iberian League gunman with three .45 slugs that sent him crashing into a wall.

Recovering from his near-brush with death, James sprang to his feet to see Katz polish off the last of his targets, and then McCarter appear in the doorway separating the two suites. The Cockney jerked his thumb over his shoulder.

"All clear back here. Four up. Four down."

"We scored the same," Katz told his British friend. "Any survivors?"

McCarter said no. "Think that's the lot of them?"

But before either Katz or James could reply, a fresh wave of gunfire erupted in the corridor outside the suites.

"Guess not," McCarter said, answering his own question.

7

"I want to go with the others," Luis Roa insisted as eight members of the Iberian League assault team vanished around the corner and out of the stairwell, then hurried down the hallway of the Hotel Plaza, preparing to launch their attack. "I don't want to miss the excitement."

"Don't be a fool because your ass doesn't sit right," cautioned Roa's friend, Pablo Pena, in a tone one notch above a whisper. "Stop fidgeting. There will be plenty of time for excitement. Use your head, Luis. If more of us participate in the first phase of the strike against the Americans, then we are sure to get in one another's way, and that could be very dangerous. No?"

"Yes," Luis Roa said. "But . . ."

"But what? Don't tell me you're worrying about losing the bonus money we have been promised?"

Roa bobbed his head. "Of course. And why shouldn't I be? But there is more. You saw the same as me on stage today how important it is to Vera and the others for us to do a good job. God, I don't want to wind up shot in the head like Roberto Conejo. I never saw so much blood in my life, not even at the cinema."

"Ha," Pena said. "If the only thing bothering you is what became of Conejo this afternoon, don't give it another thought. The idiot Conejo brought that misery on himself by not obeying orders. His problem, not ours. We were told to wait here inside this stairwell and stay out of sight until the enemy has been hit with our first wave of firepower and we are clearly in command of the situation. Only then are we to leave our position and move in. If those instructions are sufficient for the rest of our team concealed in the primary stairwell at the opposite end of the corridor, then those orders are fine for us, too.

"Don't be so anxious. If we only get to mop up the mess the advance party has created, I don't care. So much the better for us. That way we can empty our weapons into men already dead, and not have to worry about them shooting back at us. Have you thought about that?"

"Well," Roa began.

"I thought not. But think about it. We don't know how the Americans will react to our attack. Hopefully, we will surprise them and kill them all at the same time, but if some of us are meant to die before that eventual conclusion, then I would just as soon it not be me or you." He smiled and gave a soft punch to Roa's arm. "Can't spend that bonus if we're dead, Luis, eh? So we will follow orders, and later tonight we will find an imaginative way of spending some of our money."

Pena stopped speaking and risked a fast glimpse around the corner of the hallway, wondering what was taking so long. He relaxed when he saw that all was well. American investigators had taken two suites at the hotel and, as Pena looked on, he could see one of his Iberian League brothers knock at the door of the suite nearest to their hiding place and begin talking, in Spanish no less, to the Americans inside.

Satisfied, Pena ducked back into the stairwell and said to Roa, "Get ready. This is going to be the easiest ten thousand pesetas you ever made."

"We'll see," Roa, ever the pessimist, said, and was about to say more when a small explosion rumbled down the corridor and into the stairwell like a solitary clap of thunder.

That was immediately followed by the sound of automatic-weapons fire; not all of it, Pena's trained ear detected, came from the guns of the Iberian League strike force. "See?" he said to his friend. "What did I tell you? The Americans are fighting back!"

Panic flashed across Roa's face. "So what do we do? This changes everything."

"It changes nothing. We stay here in the stairwell until we are certain it is safe for us to join the attack. Until then we stay put. Don't worry, though. We outnumber the Americans more than two to one. They don't have a chance."

But the more Pena listened to the exchange of gunfire spilling from the battleground of the Americans' suite, the more concerned he became that something had gone terribly wrong. Unlike Roa and himself, who were armed with the light and short Model LC CETME assault rifles, the eight Iberian Leaguers launching the attack were all using submachine guns.

So where was all the noise that many SMGs firing at once would make? Something was definitely not right.

Then as quickly as it had started, the shooting stopped, and the eerie silence in its wake was enough to cause a wave of nausea to sweep through Pena's stomach. "I don't know," he commented.

"Now what?" Roa asked. "You can hear for yourself. There is no shooting. We have won. The fight is over. Come, we must hurry to the Americans' suite to at least say we saw their dead bodies. Otherwise, our getting paid the bonus is not guaranteed."

With that, Roa jumped from the stairwell and began moving at a trot down the plushly carpeted hallway. Pena swore under his breath at the actions of his impetuous friend but left the protection of the stairwell and began chasing after Roa, noting as he did that the five Iberian League troopers stationed in the stairwell at the opposite end were also moving in.

There were several other suites on the floor, but if any of them were occupied, the guests inside were not advertising the fact. Just as well, Pena thought, catching up to Roa. The last thing he needed was to waste time or bullets gunning down some curious bastard for opening a door.

"Hurry," Roa urged. "At this rate we will be the last ones there!"

Roa and Pena were ten meters from the gaping entrance to the suite where the Americans were trapped when the first of the pair's compatriots charged through at a dead run, only to emerge a millisecond later to the tune of a submachine gun that practically cut the IL man in two. Doubled over in agony, their gutshot friend fell in a writhing heap, screaming at the top of his lungs and doing a lousy job of keeping his insides where they belonged.

"Oh, my God!" Roa stuttered.

"Later," Pena barked.

Pena pulled Roa around by the shoulder, and the two ran for their lives.

RAFAEL ENCIZO and the latest addition to the threat offered by the Iberian League attack force met briefly at the doorway. The astonished Spaniard's eyes turned to saucers when he came face-to-face with the Cuban, the unexpected encounter made even more frightening by the Heckler & Koch MP-5 machine pistol Encizo held.

So shocked was the Spanish gunman at walking into a trap that he almost forgot the familiar weight of his own submachine gun. In the fraction of a second it took him to remember his weapon, though, his forgetfulness cost him his life. The Cuban warrior's MP-5 spoke, and the dumbstruck IL assassin perished on his feet.

"Looks like the party's only half over," Manning said, snapping off a single shot with his .357 Eagle as another of the Iberian League killers presented himself as a target in the doorway. The Canadian's aim was true, and the enemy gunman made his exit from the world leaking air and red muck from a wound in his chest.

No new hitmen showed themselves as Manning's target hit the floor. Just then McCarter came running back into the room from the adjacent suite, quickly exchanging the 9 mm Hi-Power in favor of his Ingram MAC-10.

"Well?" the Cockney asked, watching Encizo crouch and carefully examine the corridor outside for more Iberian League gunmen. "What's the weather like?"

"Raining enemy forces in both directions," Encizo said. "Three to our left, two to our right. The trio are heading straight past Calvin and Yakov. Look out!"

Encizo ducked back into the suite as James and Katz dealt with their allotment of escaping thugs by playing an Uzi/Colt Commander duet to bring the gunmen down. In a matter of seconds the shooting stopped, allowing Encizo to issue an update on his last report.

"All's quiet on the eastern front."

"Which leaves the best for the yobbos heading west," McCarter announced, checking the hallway just as the two surviving members of the Iberian League hit squad reached the stairwell door. "Don't wait up for me," the Briton commented to his partners, and then he was gone, rushing from the suite, chasing after the fleeing men.

"Oi!" McCarter shouted as he ran. "Oi! Slow down!"

Luis Roa, bringing up the rear, reacted to the sound of McCarter's voice with a 3-round burst from his CETME assault rifle, hoping somehow to frighten away the madman running at him down the corridor. But the effort was wasted. The poorly aimed shots missed Roa's target altogether and, instead of prompting the madman to turn on his heels and disappear, the opposite was true. Now the madman was coming at him faster than before, besides firing his own weapon in retaliation.

Shrieking an unintelligible oath to his ancestors, Roa leaped from the hotel's corridor and into the section of the stairwell where Pablo Pena had already taken refuge. The trouble was that the damned stairs went up, not down.

"My God! What now?" Roa moaned. "How do we get to the lobby from here?"

"Stupid question," Pena replied, climbing the stairs as though there was a Guinness record riding on his effort. "We don't."

McCarter reached the stairwell in time to hear the beat of frantic feet pounding on the bare steps. There was the noise of a door slamming open, and the sound of footsteps ceased.

Then Manning and Encizo caught up to McCarter. Encizo spoke first. "What's up?"

"They are," McCarter said. "They took to the roof."

"Right," Encizo said, hurrying back in the direction of their battle-zone suites. "I'll tell James and Katz. Maybe there's another way up."

"Guess that leaves us," Manning said after Encizo was gone.

"No sweat." McCarter started up the stairs. "We can handle it."

"I knew you'd say that," responded the Canadian, and then he was climbing, too.

Halfway to the roof the Phoenix duo were alerted by the unmistakable sound of autofire filtering into the stairwell from above, to be immediately replaced by the cries of a hysterical female.

"Crikey!" McCarter swore.

Throwing caution aside, McCarter and Manning tore to the top of the stairwell, came to an open doorway and saw at once the elements of the deadly drama enacted before them. The roof of the Hotel Plaza was bordered by ornate balusters of white stone, with upper rails composed of the same material. Additional safety for the hotel's guests was provided by wrought-iron grillwork embedded in the rails.

The body of one of the male guests was floating facedown on the surface of the Plaza's rooftop swimming pool. A liquid cloud of pink surrounded the body, which was rocked back and forth in the water by gentle waves.

Next to the pool were the Iberian League killers McCarter had chased upstairs, and held prisoner between them was the woman McCarter and Manning had heard from below. Out of her mind with horror and grief, the bikini-clad female was staring in disbelief at the body in the pool, desperately struggling to free herself so she could jump into the water.

Without taking his eyes off the killers or their prisoner, McCarter said to Manning, "What do you think, mate?"

"If we step out onto the roof with our guns, the woman won't stand a chance. They'll kill her for sure."

"You're right. And that means one of us has to go out there looking unarmed and try to talk them into letting her go—a nice trick, seeing how neither one of us poor sods speaks Spanish. Still," McCarter said, letting his MAC-10 hang free by its lanyard while bringing out the Browning Hi-Power once again, "a man's gotta do what a man's gotta do. Good luck."

Manning grumbled and slipped his .357 Eagle out of sight into the shoulder holster beneath his coat. "Why me?"

McCarter held up the Browning. "'Cause I'm as good with this as you are with a rifle."

"We'll argue about that later," Manning said, then hollered out for the two Iberian League gunmen not to shoot as he raised his hands high above his head and stepped from the stairwell onto the roof.

Concealed inside the enclosed landing at the top of the stairwell, McCarter took a deep breath and exhaled slowly, clearing his mind, fixing the aim of his Browning on the CETME-wielding rifleman who had fired at him downstairs, carefully studying the reactions of both enemy gunmen as Manning captured their attention.

"Don't shoot," the Canadian hollered to the pair, waving his arms above his head for the killers' benefit. "I'm not armed."

The gunman locked in the Hi-Power's sights swung his rifle around to bear on Manning, all the while maintaining an awkwardly vicious grip on the arm of his lady prisoner. McCarter tensed, his trigger finger itching to see what the killer would do.

"Don't . . . don't come any more near to us," the nervous rifleman ordered in halting, heavily accented English. "Stay away, or we will shoot the woman dead."

"Now," Manning said calmly, relieved to be understood, "we all know that shooting the woman is not the answer to your problems. Keeping her alive, on the other hand, has everything to do with this unfortunate situation. Right now, she's the only thing that's keeping *you* alive. Kill the woman, and you'll be dead meat . . . just like your friends downstairs."

Manning took another step forward, and the thug he was talking to yelled as loud as he could, "No! I will do as I say." His eyes flicked to his CETME-armed companion. "We both will. I swear."

"Nonsense," Manning said, inching ahead a bit more. "The woman is your protection. Kill her, and you kill yourselves, and I'm sure you don't want that."

"Never mind what we want," the gunman insisted. "Back away. Get off the roof and leave us alone."

Manning shook his head. "I'm afraid I can't do that."

"You can and you will." The second man spoke for the first time, his English considerably better than his friend's. He twisted the business end of his rifle around until it was pointed at the side of the woman's head. "Go back downstairs the way you came, or we shoot the woman now!"

Manning could tell the threat was genuine. The woman was dead unless he obeyed the order now. "All right. All right. I will leave the roof," he said, judging from the more than twenty feet separating him from the Iberian League pair that it would be impossible to get to them before the woman was shot.

Manning knew McCarter would be able to tag one of the hoods with his Browning, but trying to peg both of the killers before the woman got a bullet in her brain was stretching their luck beyond the breaking point, not to mention that of the woman. No, Manning concluded, if they were going to get away with pulling a rabbit out of this hat, they were going to need some kind of distraction.

"¡Manos arriba!" Encizo commanded the two killers from the opposite end of the roof.

Distracted for a heartbeat, each of the killers gave his attention to the sound of Encizo's voice. The rifle pressed against the woman's skull wavered and withdrew, pointing at empty space. Manning's hands dropped, his right one slapping gun leather, reaching for his Magnum.

McCarter's Browning cracked once, then twice, the shots coming so quickly after each other that there was no way to tell them apart. Hit by both 9 mm bullets, the East-Ender's handpicked target jerked off his feet as though drawn by invisible wires, twin side-by-side holes appearing over his heart. The man screamed and lost his rifle, then toppled into the pool.

The last gunman turned, reaching to keep his tenacious hold of his prisoner as she fought to pull from his grasp. He snarled and prepared to shove the bore of his assault rifle to her head again.

Manning's .357 came to life before the din from McCarter's two shots had died. Three times the Canadian's Eagle fired, all of the semiautomatic's Magnum-sized eggs striking home, hitting the stunned Iberian League gunman in the chest, neck and center of his forehead. He dissolved in a crimson spray that continued pumping long after the gunman was dead.

Manning removed his coat and draped it over the shoulders of the woman, who was now standing at the edge of the pool, weeping silently and unaware of anything but her loss. McCarter emerged from the stairwell and crossed to the Canadian, getting to Manning just as Encizo, James and Katz did the same.

"Thanks for the assist," Manning told McCarter, then commented to Encizo, "And that goes for you, too."

"We were fortunate," the Cuban replied. "There was a second stairwell at the end of the hallway that let us reach the roof from a direction our foes weren't expecting."

"Yeah," James told Encizo. "That's one surprise they'll never forget."

8

Fernando Campos hung up and ran a hand through his silver hair before turning to his associates, José Mantanez and Eduardo Vera. "So," he commented dryly, "that's quite an unexpected turn of events."

Mantanez tried to conjure up the worst scenario he could imagine. "Don't tell me the men we sent to the Hotel Plaza let one of the American investigators escape?"

"Worse," Campos replied, opting to dispense with any guessing games. "Our contact informed me that all five of the U.S. investigators are still alive."

"What?" Mantanez practically choked on his Scotch and cola. "Alive? All of them? That's impossible. There must be some mistake. Perhaps our men were delayed and the attack has simply been postponed?"

"No," Campos said. "We have always found our contact to be a reliable source of information, so why doubt it now? The strike was launched as scheduled, but didn't go as planned. The investigators from the United States proved to be more formidable adversaries than we anticipated."

"How many Iberian League casualties are we talking about here?" Vera inquired.

"Fifteen fatalities," Campos said. "We lost them all."

Mantanez sputtered and poured an extra dollop of Scotch into his drink. "This is too much, gentlemen. Too much. I realize this was the first such venture for these men, but I clearly don't see how all of them could have met their deaths."

"I think it's rather obvious," Vera indicated, annoyed at Mantanez's reaction to the news of the Iberian League's defeat. "We were careless. We allowed the fact that we knew the enemy's location in Madrid to lull us into thinking it would be an easy task to eliminate them. Now we know we were wrong."

"Yes," Mantanez added, unable to disagree, "but at the cost of fifteen men?"

"If they were defeated so handily by our opponents," Vera said, "then perhaps we should congratulate ourselves that fifteen men were all we lost. If the U.S. investigative team emerged unscathed from the incident, while all our people were killed, then it probably wouldn't have mattered if we sent twice that number."

Mantanez drained the rest of his drink and was grateful for its warmth. "Surely, you can't be serious?"

"But I am," the eldest of the three Iberian League leaders stated. "Not enough planning went into our strike at the hotel. Without knowing more about the Americans, we depended on outnumbering them to see us through to victory. Now we know we made a mistake." Vera shifted his gaze to the baldheaded Mantanez. "I'll grant you it is a costly mistake, but not too far down the road. We will put what we learned from our minor setback today to ensure it doesn't happen again.

"Up until now the Iberian League pretty much sailed on trouble-free waters. Not one of our men has suffered so much as a scratch. That kind of success breeds a dangerous complacency. In all honesty, my friends, I doubt that it occurred to any of our people hitting the hotel that they might actually lose their lives. Most of them probably went into the strike thinking themselves invincible."

"With fifteen dead," Mantanez decided, "that is one myth they are bound to rethink."

"And for that," Campos said, "I suppose we owe the U.S. investigators a debt of gratitude. By making our men aware of their mortality, of the risks involved in Iberian League membership, they will dedicate themselves all the more fiercely the next time they meet the American team."

"Yes," Mantanez protested, "but fifteen men? Just when the Iberian League is finally getting off the ground, the last thing we want is to make do with shortages."

"I never suggested we would have to," Campos pointed out. "So long as the government keeps more than twenty percent of the population unemployed, we won't have difficulty replenishing our troops."

"True," Mantanez reluctantly agreed, "but what about the expense of hiring new recruits, not to mention the money wasted on the fifteen who were killed? I never relished throwing good money away."

"Be sensible, José," Vera chastised. "No one said anything about throwing money away. What Fernando is talking about is merely investing more of our working capital now to circumvent greater expenditures in the future, which is what we will be facing if Spain's entry into the Common Market remains intact and unchallenged by us.

"It will be far less expensive for us to replenish the ranks of the Iberian League now than to deal on a competitive basis with foreign manufacturers at a later date. Our economic survival is at stake here, and I, for one, don't care how much we have to spend right now to ensure that the government accedes to our demands."

Mantanez, who never ventured far from a bar when his nerves got the best of him, poured himself another drink, this one practically all Scotch, with barely a trace of cola. He dropped a lone ice cube on top of the liquor, then downed a third of the glass in a single noisy gulp. "All right," the bald executive said, "so we will turn to our cash reserves to finance the hiring of new recruits. That still leaves us with several problems."

"Such as?" Campos asked.

"The Iberian League members who sat out this strike," Mantanez said. "They are sure to be disturbed about what happened to their friends."

"I should hope so," Eduardo Vera said. "But more than being upset, they will count themselves lucky that they didn't participate in the ill-fated strike."

"Then you don't think we will have trouble getting them to take up arms against our enemies again?"

"Absolutely not," Vera told Mantanez. "You saw how they were with me today at the theater. I had them eating out of my hand, as if they were a pack of trained dogs. The only thing I didn't have them do was roll over and play dead."

"The fifteen men we sent to the Hotel Plaza took care of that trick," Mantanez said sourly, then added, "But what you say is true, Eduardo. Your speech at the theater this afternoon even brought a lump of emotion to my throat."

"And mine," Campos seconded.

"Exactly," Vera agreed. "And if I could work them up once, I can do it again. Such manipulation of our followers is child's play. True, we are paying for their loyalty, but so long as they dance when we call the tune, they are no more than puppets with us pulling their strings.

"They get excited when we speak to them because they see our cause as noble and just; never mind bringing economics into the picture. To them the Iberian League represents Spain's only chance for surviving the onslaught of a rash government policy that cares little, if at all, for what is really beneficial for Spain as a whole. They turn to us for guidance, and we won't disappoint them. Once they have been made to view the defeat at the Hotel Plaza in its proper perspective, the Iberian League will emerge stronger than ever."

Campos motioned to Mantanez. "You said we had several problems to consider. What else were you thinking of?"

Mantanez drained the rest of his drink and set the empty glass on the bar. "The investigative team from America, of course. Or have you conveniently forgotten that they still pose a threat to our organization?"

"I'm sure none of us has put the five investigators from Washington on the back burner of neglect," Vera replied, speaking for Campos. "They bested our men in combat, but that was before we knew the extent of their capabilities under fire. Now that we are more aware of their skills, the outcome of the Iberian League's next confrontation with the five will be decidedly different from the first."

"Perhaps so," Mantanez said, not altogether convinced. "But don't forget the conditions under which our superior-numbered force was defeated. We hit the American team by surprise, and they were still able to hang our asses out to dry. Now that we have hit them and failed, they are certain to be on their guard."

"Let them," Vera said, unconcerned. "For all I care, they can sleep with their eyes open. That still doesn't mean that getting to them again is impossible. Eventually they will be ours, and not by some hasty cure-all of a plan scribbled on the back of an envelope. We were in too much of a hurry, and that cost us. Next time will be different."

"Has our contact indicated that our opponents have a weakness we could exploit?" Vera wondered.

"None," Campos confirmed, "except possibly we can concentrate on eliminating the senior member of the group, then work our way down from there. Which may not be such a bad idea. Besides being on the heavy side, I am told the old man has only one arm.''

"What?'' Mantanez asked. "The American team is led by a cripple?''

"So it would appear,'' Campos said.

Mantanez smiled. "That's it, then. Take down the old man, and if he is the one calling the shots, then the efficiency of the others may just disintegrate. Heaven knows how the men we lead would manage on their own.''

"And how can we argue with that?'' Campos said, just as Mantanez swore.

"Damn!''

"Now what?'' Campos asked.

Mantanez held up an empty bottle. "We're out of Scotch.''

9

Comisario Diaz made no attempt to disguise his anger as he and his backup of six plainclothes officers of the Cuerpo General de Policía arrived at the Hotel Plaza. Wearing a pale blue custom-made suit, a matching shirt with button-down collar and a narrow white tie, Diaz pushed his way past the bomb-blasted entrance to the first of the Phoenix team's suites, casually observing the bodies of the dead terrorists still littering the floor.

Diaz ordered his men to wait outside, then crossed to where Katz and the others were conversing among themselves in one corner of the room.

"I was afraid something like this would happen, Señor Feldman," Diaz said to Katz.

"And why is that, *comisario*?" Katz asked, unaffected by the Spaniard's harsh stare. "You should have warned us if you knew the service at the Hotel Plaza was so poor. That way my partners and I could have avoided this confrontation with the hotel staff, and gone about our investigation undisturbed."

"Do not make light of what has happened, Señor Feldman, I warn you." Diaz's lips scarcely moved as he spoke. "You may have my government's permission to conduct your investigation in my country, but that does not give you and your men the right to conduct a private war in the heart of Madrid."

The Israeli calmly lit a cigarette, but did not offer Diaz one. The time wasn't right for treating the man as an equal. "I accept your warning...now I give you mine. Don't you confuse your duties as a police officer with telling us how we are to conduct our investigation. I will not tolerate it."

Diaz smirked. "Who are you to tell me what you will or will not tolerate?"

"I could ask you the same question," Katz replied. "But if you really want an answer, you're knocking at the wrong door. I suggest you check with your immediate supervisors. If that doesn't satisfy your curiosity, then I suggest you conduct your quest a little higher along the chain of command.

"We had nothing to do with instigating this 'private war' at the hotel, and you know it. My men and I were attacked, and we defended ourselves. Unfortunately, for those trying to kill us, we were better at the game than they were."

Diaz backed away from Katzenelenbogen's icy glare and chose instead to devote his attention to the deplorable state of the suite. "This room will have to be completely redone, and the condition next door is much the same. The corridor outside both suites is in shambles—bullet holes in every direction, plus every imaginable stain ruining the carpeting. In addition, I am informed that the hotel's rooftop swimming pool must be drained and refilled because the hotel's guests may object to bloody water."

McCarter couldn't refrain from speaking out. "Are you in law enforcement or bleedin' interior decorating?"

"And are you and your associates investigators or butchers?" Diaz countered. "You will forgive my ignorance, gentlemen, but I fail to understand how you can expect to get to the bottom of the Iberian League's terrorist activities by slaughtering all of your suspects."

"We weren't given much choice," Manning said. "To hear you describe it, our big mistake was not to invite the Iberian League gunmen to sit down for a chat and tell us what they knew. Well, that kind of criminal-coddling attitude may work from your side of the street, but from where we're standing that's the surest ticket going to an early grave. That wouldn't help our investigation one bit because it's hard as hell to accomplish much when you're stretched out in a coffin."

Diaz would not be swayed. "I am afraid you will never convince me that this carnage could not have been prevented."

"We all have our crosses to bear," James said. "Yours seems to be coming up with asshole theories on how to react when some clown shoves a gun in your face. Forget that noise. It's a dead-end issue, so far as we're concerned. Besides, unintentionally or not, I think you're conveniently overlooking an important aspect of our showdown with the Iberian League."

"Which is?" Diaz asked.

"Namely this," James explained. "Our bout with the IL bad guys here at the Plaza wouldn't have happened if someone hadn't tipped off the Iberian League where we were staying.''

Diaz's face darkened with rage. "What madness is this? You're actually accusing members of the Cuerpo General de Policía of complicity in the Iberian League assault? Is that what you are doing? And what proof do you have to back up such ridiculous nonsense?''

"We didn't exactly ride in a ticker-tape parade from Torrejon air base," James pointed out.

"And I don't recall sprinkling bread crumbs behind me once we reached the lobby," Encizo added. "This hotel has more than one hundred rooms and eighteen suites, yet the Iberian League couldn't have found us any faster if someone had provided them with a map and we'd left our doors open. No, the Iberian League knew where to find us, all right, and they damn well didn't get their directions from us.''

"That will be enough," Diaz insisted, checking his watch. "The hour grows late, and I am not inclined to listen further to whatever fantasies you may entertain regarding the sanctity of my department. I must request that such outlandish notions be put to rest.

"I cannot explain how the Iberian League knew to find you at the Hotel Plaza.... I only know they did not secure that privileged information from any of my men. That being so, we must decide what we are to do with you this evening. Have you made arrangements yet concerning accommodations at another of Madrid's hotels?''

"That won't be necessary," Katz supplied. "We'll be spending the night here—in different rooms, of course, but at the Hotel Plaza nonetheless.''

"That could cause a problem," Diaz said. "After the extensive damage the hotel has sustained due to your encounter with the Iberian League, the management has expressed a keen desire to have the five of you vacate the premises. Under the circumstances, I find the management's wishes justified."

"I'm sorry to hear that," Katz said, "because we're not changing hotels; and if management has a problem with our decision, then I will leave it to you to sort it out. We have enough to keep us busy while we conduct our investigation without worrying about switching hotels."

"Be reasonable, Señor Feldman," Diaz said. "For whatever reason, the Iberian League knows where you are staying. Surely, by remaining at the Hotel Plaza, you present the terrorists with an open invitation to attack you here again."

"Not if you post your men in and about the hotel to keep watch," Katz indicated.

"That is madness," complained Diaz. "I cannot subject my men to such a menial assignment. They are highly trained police officers."

Katz smiled. "Yes, well, until our investigation is completed, it won't hurt to have them working as an adjunct to the hotel's security staff. And if you have any objections to that," the Israeli colonel added quickly as Diaz opened his mouth to protest, "then I will ask you to wait for a moment while I place a phone call so you can argue with someone else besides me."

"That will not be necessary," Diaz said after a lengthy pause. "I will see to it that you and your men are given new rooms, and I will assign six of my men to remain here at the hotel to ensure that the Iberian League does not attack here again. I do as you ask, not because I fear any reprisals from my superiors, but because by doing so I may speed along the process of your investigation, thereby ridding my country of an undesirable element."

"And who might that be, Guv?" McCarter asked. "Us or the Iberian League?"

Diaz ignored the Briton as he said to Katz, "If there is nothing else, then I will bid you *buenas noches*."

"Thank you," Katz said sincerely. "We appreciate your cooperation, Comisario Diaz. We are as anxious to get to the bottom of this Iberian League business as you are."

Diaz crossed to the ruined doorway as he called briskly over his shoulder, "The sooner the better, Señor Feldman. I will speak to you tomorrow."

THIRTY MINUTES LATER Phoenix Force was ensconced in one of their two new suites, conversing privately while enjoying an evening meal they had ordered from room service.

"Diaz has really pulled out the stops to make us feel at home," Encizo said as he devoured a generous helping of *empanadas*, deep-fried meat-and-vegetable pies. "He couldn't resent us any more if we had him and his men scrubbing out the toilets in all the rooms."

"Not that a stint cleaning the loos wouldn't suit his capabilities," McCarter decided, drinking from an ice-cold can of Coke in between mouthfuls of *cocido*, yellow chick-peas served with boiled beef and other choice bits. "It might give him a sense of accomplishment for a change."

"David's right," James said, helping himself to a first-course plate filled with *lomo embuchado*, a long strip of loin of pork cured with garlic and paprika, and dark red mountain ham sliced so thin it was translucent. "I say let the man bitch until he's blue in the face. Diaz and his boys haven't uncovered squat on the Iberian League since the terrorists hit the Transcantabrico. We show up, and the IL crazies can't get to us fast enough. Nah, if Diaz wants to gripe about something legitimate, then maybe he ought to concentrate on the inefficiency of his own department."

"Which we can discuss with the good lieutenant colonel the next time we see him," Manning offered, launching into a meal of stuffed sole topped with a vegetable sauce. "I'm sure he'll file our observations right alongside our suggestion that somebody on his side of the fence tipped off the Iberian League that we were in Spain and staying here at the Plaza."

"Which is why I elected not to have us switch hotels," Katz said. "If the Iberian League could find us so easily here, then they could probably play tag with us wherever we chose to spend the night."

"So why leave?" Encizo shrugged in agreement. "We're better off staying put, which makes even more sense now that Diaz has six of his men stationed nearby. Not that we would ever let them do our fighting for us, but the fact that they are maintaining a high profile reduces the possibility that the Iberian League will attack us again this evening.''

McCarter raised his can of Coke in a toast. "Cheers to that."

"I'm not concerned about them launching another strike against us tonight," Katz said, sampling his baby squid cooked in its own ink, "but what disturbs me is how little we really know about our enemy. The fact that nobody heard of the Iberian League before now does prompt me to wonder whether the IL could be a front for one of the other well-known terrorist groups, like ETA or GRAPO?"

"Both the Basque ETA and GRAPO—an antifascist resistance group—would savor the kind of media hoopla the assaults on tourists visiting Spain has generated," said Manning, "but since it's unlikely either group would pass up the opportunity for such spectacular publicity, my guess sees the Iberian League as the new-kid-on-the-block contenders in an already vicious contest."

"That's how I read the bastards," Katz said. "And if we accept that the Iberian League is operating independently, then we must ask ourselves why is it so important for them that Spain pull out of the EEC?"

"Probably because if Spain doesn't pull out of the Common Market," McCarter said, "the powers that be behind the Iberian League stand to lose something, come out short somewhere along the line."

"Could be," James added. "Whatever the reason is, it involves somebody with *beaucoup* bucks to spare.

You don't fund a group like the Iberian League by taking out a second mortgage on your house."

"Exactly," Katz said. "And to find such a party I think I know just where to start looking."

"Where's that?" James asked.

Katz stabbed into the air with his fork. "The library."

10

Feeling like a couple of bookworms about to burst from overeating, Encizo and James had spent the balance of the morning camped at Madrid's largest public library, poring through any and all information they could uncover relating to Spain's entry into the Common Market. The amount of material available on the topic they were researching was enormous and ran the gamut from scholarly texts hundreds of pages long, on down to short pamphlets, magazine articles and a wealth of newspaper reports that had covered the story in detail.

Surrounded by a steadily growing pile of periodicals and books of every size and description, the two Phoenix Force soldiers sat working together at a table that afforded them an excellent view of the rest of the library. Directly across from them was the establishment's main checkout desk. To the left of the desk were the double glass front doors, while to the right was the first of many rows of books stacked uniformly eight shelves high.

A wide center aisle ran between the various assortment of titles, at the end of which a wooden staircase climbed to the library's second floor. The ground plan upstairs pretty much duplicated the one downstairs, with a railed balcony area overlooking the front desk below.

Behind James and Encizo were a pair of small rooms—one devoted to current magazines and newspapers, the other reserved exclusively for those publications' back issues. The only entry to the rooms was through separate doorways facing the front desk. Neither room had windows.

While it was true that they had come to the library to search for clues regarding the Iberian League's formation, both Encizo and James had also arrived fully prepared and equipped to defend themselves against further hostilities if necessary. Besides his dependable Colt Commander riding out of sight in shoulder leather beneath his loose-fitting sport coat, James had armed himself with an S&W M-76 subgun nestled within an unzipped nylon utility bag that he kept on the empty chair next to him. His completing and final piece of weaponry came in the form of a G-96 "Boot 'n' Belt" knife worn in a sheath attached to the shoulder rig under his right arm.

Encizo also had a nylon utility bag within easy reach that contained the stocky Cuban's H&K MP-5. In addition, Encizo wore a shoulder holster whose tenant was a Walther PPK using .380 caliber rounds.

James glanced up from the newspaper he was perusing as the front door of the library opened, and a gray-haired woman with a build like a compact car made her exit after checking out some books. James waited for the door to close behind the woman before resuming his examination of the paper.

terrorists, anarchists, hijackers and drug dealers—BEWARE!

In a world shock-tilted by terror, Mack Bolan and his courageous combat teams, *SOBs* and our new high-powered entry, *Vietnam: Ground Zero* provide America's best hope for salvation.

Fueled by white-hot rage and sheer brute force, they blaze a war of vengeance against a tangled international network of trafficking and treachery. Join them as they battle the enemies of democracy in timely, hard-hitting stories ripped from today's headlines.

Get 4 explosive novels delivered right to your home—FREE

Return the attached Card, and we'll send you 4 gut-chilling, high-voltage Gold Eagle novels—FREE!

If you like them, we'll send you 6 brand-new books every other month to preview. Always before they're available in stores. Always at a hefty saving off the retail price. Always with the right to cancel and owe nothing.

As a subscriber, you'll also get...
- our free newsletter *AUTOMAG* with each shipment
- special books to preview and buy at a deep discount

Get a digital quartz calendar watch—FREE

As soon as we receive your Card, we'll send you a digital quartz calendar watch as an outright gift. It comes complete with long-life battery and one-year warranty (excluding battery). *And like the 4 free books, it's yours*

Meet America's most potent human weapons

Mack Bolan and his courageous combat squads—
Able Team & Phoenix Force— along with *SOBs*
and *Vietnam: Ground Zero* unleash the best
sharpshooting firepower ever published.
Join them as they blast their way through page
after page of raw action toward a fiery climax
of rage and retribution.

If offer card is missing, write to: Gold Eagle Reader Service,
901 Fuhrmann Blvd., P.O. Box 1394, Buffalo, NY 14240-1394

''Is it my imagination,'' he said to Encizo, ''or are the words on this page starting to mambo?''

''Could be,'' Encizo answered, looking away from his own newspaper. ''All this fine print gets to you after a while.''

James stifled a yawn. ''So I noticed. It's times like this I thank my lucky stars I learned to read Spanish as well as speak it.''

''You and me both, amigo,'' Encizo said. ''Otherwise, I'd be going through this material all by my lonesome, and you'd be outside with Katz and the others keeping tabs on the comings and goings of the library's patrons. This way, at least, we get to divvy up the work load some.''

''Speaking of which,'' James said, ''how goes the hunt?''

''Nothing to write home about. From what I've been able to gather, the majority of the Spanish people were backing the nation's entry into the EEC right from the start, and have continued to do so.''

''Yeah, that's the impression I get from what I've read, too. Just about everyone feels and felt that signing up with the Common Market was the way to go. Support for the move wasn't unanimous, though.''

''How do you mean?'' Encizo asked.

James responded to the question by shuffling through a pile of newspapers until he located the one he wanted. ''Here it is. This was dated several months before Spain's entry became official.'' He pushed the paper across the table to his friend. ''The article I'm referring to is on page one.''

Encizo accepted the paper and quickly looked the article over. "Hmm. You're right. It's not much," he commented as he scanned the pages. "It mostly talks about the Spanish industries that would take it on the chin once the EEC move was made."

"Said industries including, but not limited to, steel, shipbuilding, olive oil, wine and fishing."

"Got it," Encizo finished the article. "But it doesn't mention any organized protests coming from the industries in opposition to the proposed Common Market membership."

"I know." James took the paper back. "There's nothing in the article to link anyone tied to the industries with the atrocities committed by the Iberian League. No concrete proof at all. Still, what it does give us is the possible connection we've been searching high and low for."

"Could be," Encizo agreed. "Especially since it would take the kind of money those industries could generate to bankroll a group like the Iberian League. But, like you said, it's nothing etched in cement."

Encizo went back to scanning his newspaper for clues when James suddenly whispered to his partner. "Something hinky here, man."

The Cuban tensed imperceptibly. "Talk to me."

James looked at Encizo, then flicked his eyes over his friend's head and back down again. "There's three dudes camping out at the railing overlooking the front desk. Came out of nowhere. All three have on ankle-length overcoats. Real intellectual types; between them, they don't look like they could read the alphabet."

"We've been here since the library opened up this morning," Encizo said. "Do you recognize any of them?"

James said no. "Why don't you see for yourself?"

"I will." Encizo shifted in his seat and made a big show of stretching, turning his head momentarily up to the second-floor railing before lowering his arms. "They're new to me, too. Where do you think they came from?"

"Beats the shit out of me," James said. "But you can bet they spell trouble. I can feel it in my bones. They remind me of somebody who's just stepped up to the firing line at a shooting gallery."

Encizo felt the hairs on the nape of his neck start to itch. Without appearing obvious about it, he pulled open the top of his utility bag. "With us as the rabbits and ducks. That's dandy. How come they haven't made a move on us yet?"

"You know how these bastards operate," James said. "They don't mind offing some joker so long as they outnumber him better than three to one. Otherwise, they just sit tight and catch dust."

"So, where's the rest of their team?"

James sensed movement out of the corner of his right eye. "Coming down the stairs right now. Nice and slow."

Encizo eased his hand into his utility bag and wrapped his fingers around his reassuring MP-5. "Three of them, I'll bet," he said without looking. "That puts the odds about right. Any preferences?"

"How about if I take the high road?" James offered.

"Done. Shall we?"

"Let's."

Moving in unison, taking their respective submachine guns with them, the Phoenix Force duo leaped from their chairs and to their feet. James brought his M-76 up to bear on the three surprised men gaping at him from behind the second-floor railing, while Rafael Encizo swung around to his left to concentrate on the approaching Iberian League trio as they came to the bottom of the steps.

James opened his mouth to order his IL targets to freeze where they stood, getting no further than the first word when the tough guy holding down the center spot screamed out a Spanish obscenity and snatched an SMG of his own from beneath his coat.

Idiot, James thought, and then he was hosing down the enemy gunman with a deadly spray of 9 mm parabellum rounds.

James stopped firing as the hotshot on the receiving end of his M-76 abruptly sprouted a half-dozen holes in all the wrong places. Blood spurted from the holes like a sprinkler gone bad. The killer's legs buckled, and he slumped forward, pressing his full weight against wooden rails already weakened by the bullets James had fired. The rails gave way, and the body was airborne, somersaulting and landing on its back with the cracking sound of a breaking branch in front of the checkout desk.

The librarian behind the desk screamed and disappeared under the counter where she was working, but James had other things on his mind, such as whether the final two clowns upstairs had sense enough to quit while they were ahead. He got his answer a millisecond later after both Iberian Leaguers produced their weapons and fell back behind the railing.

"More idiots," James muttered, rushing to his left and into a new firing position as a batch of angry IL slugs drilled through the top of the table he and Encizo had been using. Shredded paper and splintered wood flew everywhere.

Mistakenly believing that James was trying to run away, the overconfident gunman who had blasted the table to sawdust corrected his aim to make instant mincemeat of the cowardly American. But then the American did something unexpected and began pumping bullets with his subgun again. It almost made the Iberian League killer want to laugh, but that was a neat trick he couldn't pull off as a flurry of slugs from the American's Smith & Wesson shaved away the top of his skull.

Spewing a fountain of blood and brain matter, the dead gunman succumbed to the gravity of his condition and spilled over the ruined railing to land in a tangle of broken arms and legs next to the Iberian League assassin who got there first. The last killer fighting from upstairs scrambled out of range before James could zero in on him.

While James dealt with his adversaries, Encizo did the same with his. Their weapons already drawn when they came charging off the staircase, the three IL thugs were astounded to discover the Cuban warrior and his MP-5 subgun waiting to greet them.

The killer in the lead regained his composure, wildly waving his assault rifle as though he half expected

Encizo to wilt from fear at the sight of it. Encizo compromised by blowing the loser away with a triple burst of H&K lead that churned the killer's digestive tract to mush. The gunman grunted, emptied his bowels and began thrashing in place, learning the steps to the dance of the dead. His two pals hop-skipped it in opposite directions, vanishing down separate aisles in the library before Encizo could nail either of the pair.

The Iberian League gunman posing the greatest danger to the Cuban counterterrorist had ducked down an aisle to Encizo's right. With the chattering of James's M-76 at his back, and the head librarian's screams of fear from behind the counter, Encizo hunched over low and raced across the floor, reaching the end of the aisle his IL foe had taken just at the moment the gun-shy terrorist came dashing around the corner.

The Cuban and Spaniard collided with enough force to send both men spilling to the floor, their submachine guns skittering out of reach. The Spaniard lashed out and with the heel of his palm struck Encizo on the side of his head. Encizo reeled, lights exploding behind his eyes, vaguely aware that the man was making another bid at clobbering him senseless.

Encizo brought his left hand up and locked it around the descending wrist, preventing the Iberian Leaguer from inflicting more damage. Simultaneously Encizo's right fist flew up and over, crashing into the middle of his enemy's face, smashing the nose to a squishy pulp that made the killer howl.

The injured assassin twisted, breaking Encizo's hold on his wrist and pushing away. He staggered to his feet and wiped his sleeve across his bleeding face. The man's broken nose was already swollen to twice its normal size, and the touch of his sleeve was agony. Even so, he couldn't resist sputtering angrily in Spanish. "You will die for the outrage of disfiguring me, I promise you!" he proclaimed in a voice rich with bloody congestion.

"Some promises are harder to keep than others," Encizo advised, taking a long step in reverse when the hitman produced a wickedly gleaming double-edged knife.

With no way to reach for his Walther PPK before he wound up playing unwilling host to the IL hoodlum's blade, Encizo went for the next best thing: his right hand flashed to the leather thong around his neck and swiftly removed the A. G. Russell "CIA letter opener" attached to it just as the killer lunged forward with his knife.

Encizo twisted out of the way, sidestepping the on-rushing blade and mentally breathing a sigh of relief as the blade missed him and stabbed with a thunk into a thick tome with a gold and silver spine. The knife lodged between the pages of the book, and before its owner could pull the blade free, Encizo retaliated by driving the business end of his dagger into the assassin's chest.

Constructed of fiberglass and nylon, but tough as metal, the weapon Encizo wielded plunged between the enemy's ribs and wormed its way into his heart.

The killer gasped, his eyes almost popping from their sockets.

Encizo yanked the knife loose, and the man gurgled something unintelligible, sinking to his knees and into the puddle he was making. Encizo left the killer pumping red wax onto the floor, then retrieved his MP-5 and set off in search of his final IL adversary.

Calvin James was debating whether he should help take out Encizo's three killers or go upstairs to combat the last man on his original hit list when gunshots and screams coming from the second floor made the decision for him. Racing as though he had a couple of bloodhounds chomping at his heels, the former SWAT team member hit the library's stairway at a dead run, taking the steps two and three at a time.

Reaching the top of the stairs, James arrived in time to witness his overcoated opponent send a barrage of bullets skimming over the heads of several library patrons struggling to escape the madman with the gun. James shouted, and the killer turned, ignoring the cowering patrons as he grinned maniacally and opened fire on James with his Star Model Z-62 SMG.

But the hardcase from Chicago was no easy target, a disconcerting fact the Iberian League gunman discovered as James dropped to the floor, rolled to the right and came up out of the roll with his S&W M-76 blitzing a hot trail of destruction through the killer's midsection. The Phoenix pro's foe let his Z-62 slip from his fingers as he curled into a squirming ball of pain and immediately started to expire.

A cry of terror coming from downstairs prompted James to venture a hurried glance over the bullet-shattered railing. What he saw below sent a chill of dread tingling through his nervous system.

One of the three IL toughs Encizo had squared off against had a death-lock grip around the librarian's neck and was gesturing with the submachine gun in his other hand for Encizo to discard his MP-5. Rather than obey the command, however, the Cuban seemed content to wait for as long as it took for the killer to realize the hopelessness of his situation and surrender.

Recognizing a stalemate that was potentially deadly for both the librarian and Encizo, James swore under his breath, realizing that trying to shoot the gunman from upstairs would pose too much of a risk to the thug's hostage. Better, James concluded, to distract the killer long enough for Encizo to go to town with his H&K machine pistol without putting the librarian in any greater danger than she already was.

What to use for the distraction, though? Then James happened to notice a wooden pedestal to his left, upon which was resting a dictionary that was so large it should have had wheels. Slipping his S&W's lanyard over his shoulder, James silently went to the pedestal and hefted the huge dictionary into his arms. It weighed a ton.

James carried the dictionary back to the hole in the railing, held the mammoth volume over the head of his unsuspecting target, then let it go. The dictionary fell on the Iberian League hood like a sack of bricks dumped from an airplane. One instant the gunman was on top of the world; the next he was dead with a broken neck.

"Good shooting," Encizo called upstairs to his partner. "I thought he was going to bump off the librarian for sure."

"Me, too," James said. "That's why I threw the book at him."

11

The three cars converged at the intersection across the street from the public library, and nine Iberian League hardcases piled out. All of the terrorists emerged from their vehicles armed to the teeth. Six of their friends were already inside the library preparing to liquidate two of the investigators from America, and they were anxious to participate in the carnage.

But first they had to get past McCarter, Manning and Katz.

McCarter ducked below the protection of the parked car he was standing behind as a fusillade of bullets sought to mow him down. A few cars down, Katz and Manning were going through the same motions as the storm of IL slugs zipped by overhead, gouging a ragged pattern of holes in the side of the library building. Pedestrians ran screaming in shock from the attack.

One of the enemy gunmen sprinted ahead of the others and came running around the car Yakov Katzenelenbogen was using for cover. Having been told less than an hour before that the ''old man'' with one arm was the opposition's weak link, and now seeing him slip out of sight, the assassin was only too happy to get the ball rolling by committing the first verified kill of the day. Unfortunately for the overzealous gunman, Katz was into racking up a few points, too.

As the sprinting Iberian Leaguer cleared the bumper shielding his primary objective, the Israeli commando opened fire with his Uzi. The Phoenix team unit commander's 9 mm persuaders worked like a charm to convince the killer to stop dead in his tracks; then to experience having his belly zipped open by a burning streak of flaming lead. Finally he was persuaded to die. The last part proved the easiest.

If that demonstration failed to convince the rest of the gunmen that launching a frontal assault on the library wasn't such a good idea, the subsequent response to the attack by Manning and McCarter definitely brought that conclusion to mind. Firing from separate positions—the brawny Canadian going for the gold with his Desert Eagle .357, the Briton relying on his Ingram MAC-10—the Stony Man pair quickly set their sights on two of the terrorists leading the pack.

Three Magnum-sized eggs cracked through the belly of Manning's target, sending a flash of fire blossoming along the man's midsection. The gutshot killer released his grip on his submachine gun, and spent his last few seconds watching a sticky flood spill through his laced-together fingers. Long before the show was finished, his eyes fluttered to show the whites, and he sank to the ground.

The object of David McCarter's attention caught five 115-grain flat-nosed projectiles from the Brit's Ingram to the accompaniment of a universe of pain that bombed its way through his nervous system. The

Iberian League hoodlum stumbled, skidding to his knees on the rough asphalt, his right index finger spasmodically locking around his submachine gun's trigger and randomly emptying the 30-round magazine of his weapon into the bodies of two of his comrades. By the time his SMG's well ran dry, the hapless duo on the receiving end of his indiscriminate assault were sprawled on the pavement next to him; the three of them participated in a faultless portrayal of playing dead for keeps.

In less than sixty seconds five enemy gunmen had perished—a sobering fact that prompted all but one of the four remaining terrorists to wonder why in the hell they had allowed themselves to be conned into thinking that the U.S. team was a bunch of helpless pushovers. That was a puzzle they were still trying to work out as they performed an awkward about-face and, firing over their shoulders to cover their retreat, attempted to return to their cars and escape.

The lone IL assassin, blindly determined to destroy his foes at any cost, ignored the flagrant cowardice exhibited by his compatriots and pressed on toward his objective. Let his friends run and hide. Who needed them? The enemies of the Iberian League had to be stopped. They had to die . . . even if that meant killing them all by himself.

Twenty-seven yards from the automobile McCarter was using as a buffer between him and IL bullets, the advancing gunman quit firing and produced a PO-111 hand grenade from his pocket. Of Spanish manufacture, the PO-111 was roughly 4.2 inches long, just over two inches wide and weighed about a pound. A fragmentation coil of metal was wrapped around the minibomb's plastic body.

McCarter looked out from behind the back of the car to see his onrushing opponent remove the PO-111's safety cap and launch the grenade in the air. Immediately recognizing the PO-111 for what it was, and with the grenade sailing at him faster than special delivery, the Cockney was on his feet and charging for the next auto down the line that shielded Gary Manning.

Pulled by a lead weight fixed to one end, the PO-111's plastic drogue unraveled. Manning turned to see McCarter diving upon him in a tackle. The PO-111's safety pin was ejected and its fuse was armed. McCarter slammed into Manning, and both Phoenix Force pros hit the ground. The PO-111 struck the side of the vehicle McCarter had hastily abandoned.

The grenade exploded, rocking the area fronting the library with an outburst of ugly noise and sending pieces of deadly shrapnel streaking for all points on the compass, but mostly in the direction of the assassin who had thrown the grenade. The PO-111 has a casualty radius of approximately twenty-four feet, and it was well within that range that the IL killer was transformed into a side of raw beef cleverly disguised as a human. Sprawled flat on his back, and staring blankly into the cold depths of eternity through the hollow sockets of his eyes, the killer's lacerated body convulsed once from head to toe, then was still.

McCarter picked himself up from atop Manning. "We can't keep meeting like this."

"I smell gas," Manning said.

"Don't blame me."

"Not you." The Canadian pointed to the black smoke that was beginning to billow from beneath the frame of the grenade-blasted wreck nearby. "It's the gas tank. She's going to blow. Come on!"

Grabbing McCarter by the shoulder, Manning, along with the Londoner, raced for the next car down where Katz was already firing on the last of the Iberian League forces to ensure the Israeli's partners safe passage to his position. Manning and McCarter reached Katz, and the three Stony Man soldiers protected themselves from the impending explosion as best they could. Then the burning fuel tank erupted with a shuddering boom, shaking the ground and sending shards of metal in a shower against the side of the library building.

The deafening roar of the detonation was starting to fade as Katz said to his men, "Is it me, or do you two ever get the feeling we're on somebody's endangered species list?"

"Only when David's around," Manning answered truthfully, glancing over the hood of the car to see the last three IL hitmen coming at them again. "Guess what, guys?"

Thinking that the exploding gas tank must have killed their adversaries or at the least left the U.S. investigative team dazed and senseless, the remaining trio of hoods abandoned their ideas for a getaway in favor of the mayhem they had intended all along. And with sirens growing louder by the second, they knew they would have to act fast.

Concentrating a heavy barrage of submachine-gun fire into a wall of lead before them, the three were confidently going through the rewarding mental motions of receiving hefty bonus payments for a job well done when an unexpected problem intruded into their plans. That unforeseen difficulty went by two names— one of them Cuban, the other American.

Appearing side by side in the library's main entrance, Encizo and James caught the Iberian League heavies looking like three clay pigeons on the wrong end of a shotgun. In a devastating duet, the MP-5 and M-76 wielded by the two freedom fighters accurately delivered a 9 mm parabellum storm that put the IL trio on ice forever. Bleeding from multiple wounds that crisscrossed their bodies in grisly patterns, the three gunmen collapsed in a lifeless heap in the middle of the street.

"Ah, that's the life," McCarter commented as James and Encizo approached. "The Iberian League spends half the day trying to get us to play Catch the Bullet, and for the most part all you two do is relax inside and have a nice read."

"I wish," James corrected. "Our friends were shooting for a clean sweep of the board."

"They hit you in the library?" inquired Katz.

Encizo nodded. "Six of them. We don't know for sure how they managed to get inside, but the head librarian did tell us there's an attic upstairs leading to the roof."

"It was a well-coordinated attack," James added. "In fact, we didn't know the IL was pulling the same nasty stunt out here with you until we heard the explosion.''

"Any luck with the research?'' Manning wanted to know.

"Some,'' Encizo answered as the first of many police cars descended upon the site of the gun battle. "But I think it will have to wait.''

"I think you're right,'' Katz agreed.

12

José Mantanez buried his face in his hands, massaging his temples to ward off the growing headache he could feel creeping up on him. "I knew when the telephone rang that it was bad news," he spoke into his palms. "My God, another fifteen of our men slaughtered."

"And so far as we know," Fernando Campos added, "not one of the investigators from the United States sustained any injuries to speak of."

Mantanez looked up. "What kind of people are these five investigators, anyway? Don't they realize they are not supposed to survive an attack when the odds are stacked so high against them?"

"Apparently not," Eduardo Vera replied. "And that is why the ranks of the Iberian League have been depleted by thirty members in less than twenty-four hours."

"And to top it off," Campos said, "the wretched team of investigators is still walking around."

"Some investigators," Mantanez complained, going to the bar for a fresh cola and Scotch. "Such a ruse is impossible to believe. I am convinced they must be working for the CIA. Who else could hope to keep such efficient killing machines under control?"

Campos arched an eyebrow. "CIA? That is strange. I was unaware you've had dealings with the Central Intelligence Agency. Why haven't you mentioned this affiliation to us before?"

Mantanez finished pouring and mixing his drink, and went straight to work polishing it off. "All right," he said in between swallows, "I admit I am guessing when I say the troublemakers are CIA assassins. But what is the difference? Thirty of our people are dead just the same."

"True," Vera said, "which tells us how foolhardy we'd be to try and take out all of our formidable adversaries at once the next time we attempt to kill them."

"What 'next time'?" Mantanez could not believe what he was hearing. "Surely we are not going to send more of our men out to be butchered?"

"Not if we can help it," Vera said. "And we can help it if we take certain precautions in advance. The problem with the so-called investigators is not going to magically vanish simply because it would serve our best interests for them to do so. They are here in Spain to do a job, which is to stop the Iberian League, and it is up to us to see that they don't succeed."

"Naturally," Mantanez said. "But how can we expect to triumph over individuals who laugh at death and get away with it? I tell you it is as though we are trying to kill off a race of supermen."

"Nonsense," Vera corrected. "They will bleed as easily as anyone else...a fact that we must prove quickly to our men if we wish to continue to maintain their confidence."

"And how do we manage that?" Mantanez asked. "This latest fiasco at the library isn't something we can sweep under the rug. I don't care what the unemployment conditions in this country are, or how much the men we hire appreciate the money we pay them. Our men aren't stupid.

"Once it dawns on them that money is very difficult to dispose of from the grave, no amount will lure them back to us. They will hang our cause out to dry so fast we won't know what hit us. And once they are lost to us, that's it. We will be on our own, with no way of putting any muscle behind our threats to the government to force Spain out of the EEC."

"Not that they have exactly been hopping to meet our demands up to now," Campos noted.

"We knew before we got the Iberian League rolling that the government wouldn't come around to our way of thinking overnight," Vera said. "So we shouldn't be overly concerned that they are dragging their heels. It's going to take time."

"Which we cannot afford," protested Mantanez as he drained his glass. "So long as the butchers from America roam free, time is on their side, not ours."

"A problem we shall remedy," Vera vowed. "But first we must come up with a way to boost the morale of our men, a way of easing the pain of another stinging defeat at the hands of our enemies."

"We want the investigators dead, and we want our people to reclaim some of their self-respect," Campos said, watching as Mantanez put together the makings for another drink. "I believe we can concoct a scheme that solves both our problems at once."

"A smooth trick if we can pull it off," said Mantanez. "What are you suggesting?"

"It is nothing complicated," Campos answered. "If we cannot seem to eradicate our foes while they are fighting as a team, then we must come up with something to force them to split up. That will reduce their overall strength and make them more vulnerable.

"Losing so many of their friends to the bullets of the investigators will rouse in our Iberian League defenders a thirst for revenge that can only be quenched by blood."

"Naturally they will want revenge," Mantanez said, fishing in a plastic bucket for a handful of ice cubes, which he dropped into his drink. "But will they risk doing what it takes to achieve it? What are you proposing?"

"This," Campos responded. "First, we give our men a taste of blood to whet their appetite for more."

"And then pit them against our five superheroes from the States," Vera said. "It is a tall order to get the five to separate, but if we can pull it off, then I think we can safely say that the Iberian League's mission will be back on schedule after experiencing this unfortunate delay."

Mantanez sipped his drink. "All right. Split and then hit. Sounds good to me, but how do we get it to happen?"

"Unless I am mistaken," Vera told the balding Mantanez, "Fernando already has something in mind."

Campos smiled and reached for the phone at his side. "Just watch me."

THE TOWERS OF SERRANOS, constructed in 1398 by Pere Balaguer to serve as a gateway to the then-walled city of Valencia, seemed a perfect location for the Weiler family to stop and take photographs.

"And look at this, Papa!" young Klaus Weiler exclaimed, reading excitedly from the colorful brochure in his hands. "It says the *torres de Serranos* also features a small maritime museum. Surely, after we have taken a few pictures, it would be worth our while to see what the museum has to offer?"

"I don't know about that," Heinrich Weiler told his son. "We only have two days remaining of our holiday, and it would be a shame to waste time on anything frivolous."

"Oh, don't tease the boy so," Brigitte Weiler scolded her husband as he brought their rented compact car to a halt beside the well-tended park across from the towers. "You know how Klaus goes mad for all things connected with the sea." She turned and said to her son, "Don't worry your head, dear. Father was only joking with you. Of course we will explore the museum. That is what we are on vacation for, no? To have as much fun as possible before we have to go home. So, worry not. After the picture-taking, it's off to the museum."

"Wait a minute. Hold on," the elder Weiler protested good-naturedly. "Maybe I don't want to see some silly old maritime museum. Don't I get a vote in the matter?"

"Not this time," Klaus laughed, and then he was following his parents out of the car and over to the tree-shaded park where the family photo session began in earnest.

Heinrich Weiler started by photographing his wife and son together, and then in separate poses, utilizing the park and the Towers of Serranos themselves as impressive backdrops for the pictures. Halfway through the roll of film, Herr and Frau Weiler traded places and repeated the same routine, taking snapshots of father and son that would soon grace the pages of their photo album back home in Trier.

Finally, with all but four of the photos on the roll preserved for posterity, Herr Weiler was lining up another interesting shot when he sensed someone next to him.

"Ja?" he said to the Spanish gentleman standing nearby, with a cotton carryall bag slung over his shoulder.

"¿Habla usted español?" the man asked.

Herr Weiler shook his head. *"Nein."*

The determined Spaniard tried again. *"¿Habla usted inglés?"*

"Ja!" Heinrich Weiler nodded, switching smoothly from German to English. "I speak a little English. How may I help you?"

"I hope you will forgive me bothering you," the Spanish stranger said in an accent that was fairly thick and difficult for Heinrich to comprehend. "But I was passing by and couldn't help noticing you were taking the photographs of your family. You are visiting Valencia on holiday?"

"Yes," Herr Weiler said. "You have a lovely city."

"Gracias. We are proud of our beautiful city. Which is why I felt I must speak to you."

"Yes?"

"It is about the photographs you are taking. It would be sad not to have some photos with the three of you in them. Much better to have everyone in the family smiling together. If you would like, I would be happy to photograph you with your wife and son."

"Really? That would be wonderful." Weiler lifted his camera strap off his neck and held it out. "I have four pictures left on the roll. Are you familiar with using a camera such as mine?"

"Do not be afraid," the man said, accepting the camera. "All cameras are my friends. Now go, take up a pose with your family, and I will use up your roll of film."

Heinrich Weiler was only too pleased to do that, hurrying over to where Brigitte and Klaus were waiting, and then smiling with his family into the camera while the Spanish gentleman quickly snapped off the last four pictures. After the final photo was taken, Heinrich started to come forward to thank the friendly stranger, when the Spaniard held out his hand for the German to keep still.

"Please," the stranger said. "You are such a warm and lovely family. May I ask you if it would be all right to shoot you with my camera?"

Heinrich Weiler glanced to his spouse and son, then promptly replied, "But of course. How can we refuse your request? You have been generous with your valuable time to photograph us; we would be honored to pose for you."

"Good," the Spaniard said, letting the Weilers' camera hang free from its neck strap while he reached inside his carryall. "Now, give me three big smiles. This won't take a second."

With his arm around his wife and son, Heinrich Weiler stood tall and waited for the photo session to end—an event that came faster than he could have dreamed as the kindly Spanish gentleman produced from his bag, not a camera as expected, but a 9 mm automatic pistol instead. Weiler opened his mouth to scream for the stranger not to fire, but the initial Largo round of the Star Superba silenced the German's voice forever.

Two shots more, and the destruction of the Weiler family was complete. The man responsible for their death dropped his pistol into his bag and crossed to where Heinrich Weiler had fallen. Somewhere in the distance a cry of alarm could be heard.

Kneeling beside the body of his victim, the murderer thrust a folded piece of paper into the dead man's hands, closing the lifeless fingers around it. Then he stood and, still in possession of the murdered family's camera, calmly made his way from the scene of the crime.

One hour later, a French family admiring the star-shaped designs of the Plaza de Cataluña in the seaport city of Barcelona were busy taking pictures of one another. They were approached by a Spanish gentleman graciously willing to photograph the family together. It was an offer the family from the town of Blois gratefully accepted.

13

"The suggestion has merit," Katz said, concurring with Encizo and James that the information they had uncovered at the library was worth further consideration. "It certainly would explain where all or part of the financial backing for the Iberian League originates from."

"That's what we thought," Encizo reported. "And if someone connected with one of the country's major industries stands to lose in the profit department because of Spain's entry into the Common Market, then maybe they figure footing the bill now for the IL wackos will save money in the long run."

"Yeah," Gary Manning said. "Like an investment in the future. But that's if and when the Spanish government elects to back out of its commitment to the EEC."

"Which we all know ain't gonna happen," James observed. "The Iberian League's all wet; they're pissing against the wind."

"Right," McCarter said, taking a drink from his ice-chilled can of Coke. "Although, how I suss it out is that the money behind the IL doesn't give a damn at this stage of the game. They probably feel they can dish it out longer than the Spanish government can take it and can afford to lose men left, right and center because bodies come cheap to people in power. They never really care who dies fighting for their cause because they always have some other poor bastard on the hook waiting to take their place.''

Encizo checked his watch. ''I wonder what's keeping our friend, the *comisario*?''

''No mystery there, mate,'' McCarter decided. ''Diaz has been walking around with blinders on since our jet touched down at Torrejon. And if he ever rolled out the red carpet for us, I sure as hell missed it. No, he'll show up soon enough, even if it's only to throw a little more aggro our way. But he won't pop by until he's good and ready.''

''Where Diaz gets off acting so high and mighty is beyond me,'' James said. ''His scorecard to date against combating the Iberian League menace rates a big fat zero.''

''You're being too generous,'' Manning said. ''Diaz may have his superiors convinced he's out slogging it for the good of the local citizens, but from where I sit his entire anti-IL campaign is an embarrassing washout. We're the ones going toe-to-toe with the terrorists, not Diaz. He and his *compadres* haven't exchanged so much as a spitwad with the Iberian League.''

''Perhaps Diaz figures that's a safer route for nim to take?'' Encizo surmised. ''If we do his job for him, then he can waltz in at the end of the song and join the victory dance.''

''I don't mind if the man wants to bask in our sunshine without getting burned,'' Katz said. ''Let him.

All I care about is completing our mission and crushing the Iberian League so that their wholesale slaughter of innocent tourists is stopped.

"Hassles go with the territory, but it would be easier to tolerate Diaz and his arrogance if I felt the man actually supported our efforts. He made it clear right from the start, though, where he stands on that issue. Nothing would make him happier if we called it quits and packed our bags to leave."

Someone knocked on the door, and James said aloud, "What do you think? Is the *comisario* finally gracing us with his presence?"

"Either that or Diaz phoned for a taxi to carry us to the airport," Manning guessed, rising from his chair and going to the door.

In the Canadian's right fist was his Eagle .357 Magnum, because, although it was true that Diaz had assigned some of his subordinates to remain on guard in and about the Hotel Plaza, Manning wasn't prepared to take unnecessary chances to prove Diaz's men were doing their job. Hard lessons learned long ago on the battlefield had taught Manning never to assume an area was safe and secure merely because someone else said so. Such careless assumptions could have a devastating price tag.

Manning reached the door and called, "Who is it?"

"Comisario Diaz!" came the angry voice from the hallway outside. "Quit playing games and open this door!"

Manning turned back to his partners. "What do you think? Should I let him in?"

James shrugged. "Might as well. We don't want to get the man upset with us."

"Heavens, no!" Manning said, unlocking the door and opening it for Diaz. "Why, Comisario Diaz. What a pleasant surprise."

Like a runaway wrecking ball looking for a building to demolish, Diaz stormed by the Canadian and into the suite. Wearing a totally new set of tailored clothes, the only thing unchanged from the last time they had seen the man was his shellacked hairstyle and the large diamond ring he wore on his left hand.

As soon as he reached the middle of the room, Diaz reared on his feet, presenting Katz with a harsh stare that had taken years to perfect. "So, Señor Feldman," he confronted the Israeli. "I see you and your friends have had a busy afternoon, wouldn't you say?"

"No more than most," answered Katz.

Diaz smirked. "How enlightening. Then you habitually conduct gunfights in public libraries and city streets? Most interesting. I am relieved to know such outlandish behavior seems a natural occurrence for you; otherwise I would suspect you and your men behaved like common criminals today."

"That's a load of crap, and you know it," James spoke up. "We were attacked, and we defended ourselves. Since when is self-defense a criminal offense?"

"Maybe what the *comisario* is telling us," McCarter jumped in before Diaz could reply, "is that he doesn't understand self-defense—not too surprising, considering the number of encounters with the Iberian League he hasn't experienced."

"Meaning?" Diaz demanded.

"That you haven't exactly set any speed records getting into the thick of things," the Londoner said. "Hanging about, dragging your bum to the ground may be how you work, pal, but not us."

"I have been wondering," Diaz told McCarter, "how it is that someone from England happens to be working in concert with a team of special investigators from the United States?"

"Takes all kinds," the Briton answered. "Which, I would imagine, explains how you became a *comisario*."

"I shall not dignify that remark with a comment," Diaz said, then turned abruptly to Katz. "Given the substantial amount of damage to life and property resulting from your escapade within, and without, the library, I am amazed you and your men were not arrested when the authorities arrived."

"Don't be disappointed," Katz said freely. "The Policía Gubernativa had every intention of arresting us."

"But?" Diaz questioned.

"But after I made a single telephone call, the officer in charge became convinced that arresting us wasn't in his best interests. Now—" the Israeli colonel leaned forward "—am I going to have to make another such call, or are you going to climb off your high horse and quite behaving like an insufferable ass?"

Diaz turned beet-red, but he soon backed away from Katzenelenbogen's challenge. "That will not be necessary, Señor Feldman," he said between clenched teeth. "We are, after all, working on the same side. No? You want to rid my nation of the Iberian League killers; the Cuerpo General de Policía desires the same. Our goals are not unlike."

"Good," Katz said. "Then we can get down to business. Did you stop by to share some particular information with us, or was the purpose of your visit simply to express your displeasure over the way we handled the IL terrorists?"

"My primary reason for coming by," Diaz stated, "was to divulge some news that I felt you were entitled to know."

"I'm listening," Katz said.

"It is the Iberian League," Diaz began. "They have been up to the old tricks again."

"More tourists murdered?" Manning asked.

"Two entire families," Diaz replied. "A German family of three was shot to death in Valencia, while another family of four, from France, was murdered in Barcelona a short while afterward. In each instance, the Iberian League claimed responsibility for the killings."

"Damn," James swore. "It's frustrating. No matter how fast we've cleaned up on the IL crazies, we've still gone too slow to stop them from offing more helpless people." He said to Diaz, "When did the latest killings take place?"

"This afternoon, with the murders being committed about sixty minutes apart."

"Which indicates that more than one Iberian League group participated in the executions," Encizo said. "Were there any reliable witnesses to be found?"

"None," Diaz admitted. "By the time anyone reached the victims, the perpetrators in both cases had already fled the scene."

"How did the Iberian League stake a claim for the hits?" Calvin James asked. "The same as with the guy they iced up in Brussels yesterday?"

Diaz nodded. "In each incident, the notes discovered with the bodies promised more deaths would follow in both cities within the next twenty-four hours unless my government heeds the Iberian League's demands to cancel its membership in the EEC."

"Thank you for this information," Katz said.

"You are welcome," the Spanish plainclothes policeman returned with the first display of cordiality he had shown Phoenix Force. "May I inquire what you and your associates' plans are, Señor Feldman?"

Katz smiled warmly. "I sincerely wish I could tell you, but there are many factors to contemplate before even I can know what our next move will be. You can rest assured, however, that I will keep you informed after I've come to a final decision." Katz gestured with the curved metal end of his hooked prosthesis and began escorting Diaz to the door. "Now, if you will excuse us, *comisario*. My men and I have much to talk about."

"Of course," Diaz said, making his exit with no further coaxing. "I hope to hear from you soon."

"So," Manning commented after Diaz was gone, "the Iberian League has opened branch offices in Valencia and Barcelona."

"Which isn't to say they've automatically pulled up stakes here in Madrid," said Encizo. "Although that may be the impression we're supposed to get."

"Could be," James decided. "My gut reaction to the latest killings says the two families were murdered not only to maintain the pressure on the Spanish government but to lure the five of us to Valencia and Barcelona as well."

"That's my reading of the situation, too," Katz confirmed. "Otherwise, I doubt the IL terrorists would go to such lengths to advertise their plans to kill more tourists within the next twenty-four hours. I believe they want to make it impossible for us not to swallow their bait."

"Naturally," McCarter said. "They'll have to expect that we're willing to do anything to prevent the additional slaughter of innocents."

"And they're right," the Phoenix team's unit commander confessed. "Not that the Iberian League wants a repeat performance of our earlier confrontations. Which is why they have lit the fuse for future terrorist activities in separate cities. They know the only way we have of covering both bases at once is for the five of us to split up—two going to one city, three of us heading for the other. Again, while doing so probably puts us smack-dab in the middle of whatever scheme it is the Iberian League's cooked up, if we don't accept their invitation, then it's a certainty more tourists will die."

"Exactly," Katz agreed. "And since we're already into the twenty-four-hour countdown established by the terrorists, it's imperative we set off for Valencia and Barcelona as soon as possible."

"Who's going to clue Diaz in to our decision?" Encizo asked with a smile.

"Ha, ha, ha," James laughed dryly. "Just 'cause our plainclothes fashion plate got religion and stopped behaving like a total ass for a couple of minutes is no reason for us to think his act is going to last."

"Fine," the stocky Cuban replied. "Just checking."

"Let's do it, then," Manning announced. "If nobody objects, I'll go to Barcelona with Calvin. Katz, you and Rafael can take Valencia, not to mention McCarter."

"Hey!" the East-Ender protested. "What am I all of a sudden? The flaming fifth wheel? What's wrong with me going to Barcelona?"

"Sorry." The brawny Canadian chuckled as he began collecting his gear. "Katz drew the short straw."

"What a wanker," McCarter grumbled.

"OUR TROUBLES ARE OVER, gentlemen," Fernando Campos informed his partners. "The nightmare of the U.S. investigators is ended. They are leaving Madrid, presumably for Barcelona and Valencia. They are on their way to their own funerals and don't even know it."

"I'll believe it when it happens," José Mantanez said. "Not before. Those five have been the source of two major defeats for the Iberian League, and I would hate to think we are merely setting ourselves up for numbers three and four.''

''Highly unlikely,'' Eduardo Vera said. ''The luck our enemies have enjoyed cannot endure forever. Stretch it thin enough, and everything will snap. Now that we have enticed our enemies into separating, I am positive we have seen the last of them.''

''I hope you are right, my friend,'' Mantanez said, ''for I can think of nothing worse than the American team surviving Barcelona and Valencia, then coming back here searching for us.''

''Your fears are groundless,'' Campos told him. ''Be patient. You will see I am right. In the meantime, you look thirsty. Please, help yourself to the bar.''

''Thank you.'' Mantanez took Campos at his word and was soon engaged in mixing his favorite drink. ''The investigators are not stupid. They must know by now we have been on to them all along.''

''What of it?'' demanded Campos. ''In a few short hours what they know or don't know won't matter to any of us.''

14

With air shuttle service between Madrid and Barcelona available every hour from seven in the morning, Calvin James and Gary Manning had no difficulty taking advantage of the *puente aéreo* flights to get to the famous seaport city.

With its mild climate, characteristically pleasant breezes and rich historical heritage stretching back more than two thousand years when the city served as an outpost of the ancient Roman Empire, Barcelona had everything a demanding tourist could desire. James and Manning, however, hadn't traveled to the capital of the province of Catalonia to enjoy the weather or to take colorful snapshots for the folks back home. Somewhere in Barcelona, Iberian League murderers were waiting to strike again against the defenseless; Manning and James were determined to stop the terrorists before they could kill again.

"So," Manning said as they contemplated the Plaza de Cataluña—the eight-pointed star-shaped site where the French family had brutally lost their lives earlier in the day. "This was as good a place as any to start looking. Where to now? Maybe the IL crazies checked into one of the area's hotels?"

"I hope not," James said, consulting a brochure he had acquired in the airport outside of the city. "Barcelona has 314 hotels altogether, offering a total of 39,797 beds. We could go through the list all the way from A to Z and not even come close to the bastards."

"And that's assuming the Iberian Leaguers are from out of town. Who's to say they're not homegrown locals who've signed on for the duration of the Iberian League's campaign?"

"Yeah, well, if that's the case," James said, "we've got our work cut out for us. If the bunch who dealt with the French tourists are locals, then straight out of the chute that gives them the home court advantage. This is their ballpark, not ours. They could be hiding anywhere."

"True," Manning agreed. "Then again, if they're like the trigger-happy crowd we've met up with in Madrid, it's unlikely the people we're searching for will be sipping wine at one of Barcelona's country clubs, or suiting up for a fast game of polo.

"Cities are like coins. There's two sides to them. Good and bad. I say our best bet for cracking this nut is to take a look now at the sort of places we wouldn't want to be in after dark. Sooner or later—sooner if we're lucky—we'll tumble onto something to help us track down the terrorists."

"Especially if, as we suspect, the Iberian League set up shop in Barcelona merely as a ploy to lure us here."

"Exactly," Manning said. "And that could mean the IL terrorists want us to find them, or at least want to have a go at removing us from the picture without

coping with Yakov and the others at the same time."
The Canadian smiled grimly as he and his lanky
American companion made their way from the Plaza
de Cataluña to where their rented Volkswagen Golf
was parked. "Who knows? Maybe the Iberian League
was stupid enough to think you and I would be a couple of pushovers if they got us away from the rest."

"I suppose it's possible," James said. "Everyone
makes mistakes."

Rather than waste valuable time to attempt to locate the underbelly of Barcelona's seamier districts,
the Stony Man duo opted for a quick solution to their
problem by hiring a taxi driver to lead them with his
cab where they wanted to go. Following the Spanish
cabbie through a maze of winding streets, the Phoenix Force pair soon found themselves in a section of
the city less frequented by the typical tourist. The task
completed to his satisfaction, the driver of the taxi
they were tailing beeped his horn once, waved his hand
in a farewell gesture out his window, then turned a
corner and was gone.

"This looks like the place," Manning said, to which
James promptly replied, "We'll see."

Depositing their Volkswagen in a private parking lot
on a small paved strip between a seedy-looking bar
and a hotel whose guests paid by the hour, James and
Manning hit the streets in pursuit of the Iberian
League's whereabouts. Although the traditional afternoon siesta from one to four was still more than
thirty minutes from drawing to a close, it was evident
at the outset of their search that certain business es-
tablishments in this part of Barcelona weren't pre-

pared to sacrifice profits simply to placate antiquated customs. Vice in all its incarnations, the Canadian and American saw, had no shortage of buyers.

Slipping through the doorway of a dimly lit bar with sticky floors and bad plumbing, James and Manning made their way over to the disinterested bartender, who was absently drying a glass with a towel. The bartender sized up the newcomers suspiciously before finishing with the glass and asking what they wanted.

"Information," James answered fluently in an accent the bartender had no trouble understanding.

The man casually picked up another wet glass and began rubbing it with his towel. "If you want news, buy a paper. I serve drinks here, not information."

James made a show of looking around the bar's interior. Except for themselves and the bartender, the only other patrons were a man and a prostitute who were animatedly going through negotiations for a horizontal date.

"Sorry to be blunt," James told the bartender with a jaunty smile, "but unless most of your customers are flies, right now you don't seem to be serving much of anything, let alone drinks. Considering your lack of clientele, I am surprised you are so negative to parting with a little information."

"How little and for how much?" the bartender asked.

James responded by requesting the price of a couple of beers. After the bartender told him the amount, James said, "Fine. My friend and I are very thirsty today, so we will buy two beers and pay you for fifty.

That will get us each a drink, with some information on the side. What do you say?''

By then the two glasses of beer were already being filled and set on the bar in front of James and Manning. "Here are your drinks."

"And here is your money," James returned.

The bartender accepted the pesetas and slipped the cash out of sight as he leaned confidentially over the bar. "Now, tell me," he said. "What is so important for you to know that you are willing to pay me to find out?"

"We are in Barcelona to do a little hunting," James said.

The bartender frowned. "Oh? Then you are in the wrong part of town. I suggest you visit our zoo."

"You misunderstand," James said. "What we plan on hunting relates to the unfortunate incident at the Plaza de Cataluña today."

The bartender nodded. "Ah, I see. The animals you seek walk upright. You are hunters of men."

"Precisely," James said.

"Killing the tourists was a despicable thing," the bartender reflected. "Everyone says so. Yet what have the deaths of a French family to do with me? Surely you don't suspect I'd involve myself in such brutality?"

"Of course not," James told the man, "but since your place of business doesn't exactly fall within the shadows cast by La Seu cathedral, I figured it couldn't hurt to inquire if you heard anything that might help us."

The bartender shrugged and continued with his chore. "Certainly not. I'm sorry. But even if I did know something, I'm not altogether sure it would be safe for me to reveal it to you. These people who murdered the French tourists are dangerous. A person's health could take a turn for the worse if the killers discovered you were assisted in your hunt."

"True," James agreed, "but not with a successful hunt. Anyone helping us would be safe and sound, and that much richer for the experience."

"Not that I know anything of value," the bartender said, "but for speculative purposes only, how much richer would a person be for putting you on your quarry's track?"

"Enough to make it worth his while," James said. "We could be talking about as much as… But why go into unnecessary details? Since your knowledge is strictly limited to what you already told us, then we had best look farther up the street. I'm sure the information won't be lost forever." He said to Manning in English, "Let's go."

The American and Canadian turned to leave as the bartender called excitedly to James, "Don't discount me so easily. I may not have the information you're looking for now, but that condition, like the weather, is subject to change. Ask about the neighborhood to learn what you are able. If the results of your expedition are poor, then be sure to check back with me. Perhaps by then I can assist you on your hunt."

"Perhaps," James said.

"Wait," the bartender cried. "What about your beers? You didn't touch a drop."

James pointed to the corner of the bar where the hooker and her potential customer were still haggling over the fee for services rendered. "They can have them. With our compliments."

And then James and Manning were out of the bar and walking up the street to the next likely stop on their tour of the neighborhood.

"Well?" Manning asked as they approached another bar that could have passed as the twin of the one they had just left. "What's the word on the barkeep? I got the feeling he was interested in our money, but really didn't have anything to sell."

"That's what I thought," James said. "Though he did invite us back if we don't find what we're looking for. No guarantees, but it gives us an option we didn't have before."

"Maybe we'll take the man up on his offer," Manning said, stepping through the open doorway and into the bar, with James following close behind.

Five bars, three seedy hotels and a couple of cafés later, the two Phoenix Force commandos were preparing to embark on the next leg of their search when James casually commented to his partner, "Don't look now, Gary, but I think our Barcelona vacation is starting to pay off."

"We're being tailed, I know," the Canadian said without turning around. "I spotted the runt trying to blend into the scenery about the same time you did— kind of short, with a beard and a shaggy head of hair."

"That's the one. He's about half a block behind us and—" Manning shifted his stance so he could determine their shadow's whereabouts without seeming obvious ''—no, hold on, he's moved into position nearer to us now. You see any sign of pals he might be running around with?''

James glanced in the opposite direction. ''Negative. But it's unlikely that the Iberian League would try nailing us with one man. That's suicide, not strategy.''

''So, let's discuss the matter with old fuzzy face,'' Manning said. ''If he's so curious about what you and I are up to, let's give him a chance to find out.''

Ignoring the fact that the suspect was continuing to draw closer, Manning and James vanished through the entrance to a windowless eatery whose advertised specialty was a stew made with a kind of white sausage. The aroma of spices and roasting meat filled the air.

''Smells good,'' James observed, moving to the side of the restaurant's doorway and out of sight of anyone passing by on the street. ''Too bad we can't stay for an afternoon snack.''

''No chance,'' Manning said, standing across from James so he couldn't be seen from the street. ''Something tells me we wouldn't make it through the first course.''

Within sixty seconds, the Canadian's prediction came true as the bearded face belonging to the man following them poked curiously through the restaurant's doorway. The shaggy-haired man pushed farther into the building, and his right hand strayed beneath his coat for a pistol stuffed into his belt. His fingers closed around the butt of the gun.

"¡No seas loco!" James warned.

But the shocked gunman was too stunned to heed the American's advice. Spinning to his right to the unexpected sound of James's voice, the IL terrorist gasped in surprise and desperately tried to withdraw his weapon. He was prevented from carrying out his plan by Gary Manning's powerful fist closing over his own, keeping his pistol in place, its barrel pointed down the leg of his pants.

"Tell the runt he's a heartbeat from singing soprano the hard way if he doesn't relax and take his hand off his gun," Manning said.

James translated the message, and the long-haired Spaniard, swearing under his breath, reluctantly obeyed the Canadian's command.

"Good." Manning removed the Iberian Leaguer's weapon, then said to James, "He's all yours. I say we escort our prize back to our car, then find someplace nice and quiet where we can all have a chat."

James smiled. "I'm sure the runt would like that just fine."

Telling their captive that they wouldn't hesitate to shoot if he tried to escape, James and Manning ushered the terrorist back outside the restaurant. Then the three of them began heading toward the Stony Man duo's parked Volkswagen Golf. They had covered no more than a third of the distance to their ultimate destination when three surly-looking strangers abruptly appeared on the sidewalk directly ahead.

"Guess what?" Manning said.

"Do I have to?" James asked.

The trio blocking their way threw open their coats, reaching for handguns concealed beneath. Simultaneously Manning and James reacted to the threat in a manner befitting members of the world's foremost antiterrorist organization, Manning bringing his .357 Eagle into play, while James filled his hand with his deadly Colt Commander.

Thinking this was an ideal opportunity to break away from his captors, the bearded terrorist shook free from Manning's grasp and turned to run, instantly regretting his short-lived flight to freedom as he collided head-on with Calvin's Colt crashing into his skull. The man felt a stab of pain exploding over his eyes, then darkness invaded his universe, and he knew no more.

As the Phoenix pair's captive sank in an unconscious heap to the pavement, James and Manning opened fire, each of them singling out the nearest Iberian League gunman. With less than fifty feet separating them from their opponents, their respective targets were difficult to miss.

First to clock out was the killer Manning had opted to dispose of. The loser was still fumbling for his autoloader when one of the Eagle's angry projectiles cracked him on the chest and kept on going, blasting through his rib cage and churning his insides. The man coughed, sputtered a stream of red bubbles from his lips, then went into death throes.

The terrorist James set his sights on managed to unleash one hastily aimed shot with his HK-4 DA semiauto, which gouged out a hole in the wall next to the black American's right shoulder. Then James's

Colt Commander got into the act and the IL gun-man's days of slaughtering innocent tourists were ended forever. Struck twice in the belly by side-by-side .45 caliber minirockets, the gutshot killer screamed and dropped his HK-4 to the ground, doubling over and collapsing in a fit to his knees. A third shot from the Commander blew the writhing man's forehead apart and sent his corpse into a last convulsive dance.

The final killer confronting Manning and James found himself in the unenviable position of having both his adversaries fire upon him at the same time. Coming so close together, it was impossible to tell one hit from the other, and the luckless gunman felt dual explosions of agony erupt from deep within his chest and through his stomach. His mind dully registering the insufferable depths of his pain, he lost his footing and ended his life hugging the cold, hard sidewalk.

"Three up. Three down," James announced, indicating the unconscious bearded man on the ground. "Let's get Sleeping Beauty to our car before more of his chums show up."

"Not this time." Manning pushed James into the protected doorway of a four-story eight-room hotel just as a fresh barrage of enemy lead threatened to mow them down on the spot.

"Damn!" James swore. "When it rains it pours."

"No argument there."

"How many more ILs are we talking about?"

"Three, possibly four," Manning answered. "Sorry the head count isn't accurate, but they didn't give me much chance for a roll call."

James cautiously prepared to fire his Colt Commander around the corner of the doorway, but quickly changed his mind after a steady stream of bullets decorated the front of the quarter-star hotel, sending bits and pieces of plaster and stone into the air. "Apology accepted," he said. "Now what?"

"Now we come up with a clever way of getting our asses out of this mess."

"Any ideas?" asked James.

"That was my question," Manning said.

James looked over his shoulder. "We could duck out through the hotel. It has to have more than this single entrance. If we do that, though, and the IL gunmen pursue us inside, then we risk putting innocent lives in jeopardy."

"Yeah, well, we sure as hell can't stay here forever," Manning said. "So far the terrorists have stuck to using handguns to try and do us in. If they decide to change tactics and start lobbing grenades at us, we're cooked. We'll be flying back to Stony Man under our own power."

"Nuts to that noise," James complained. "Tell you what. You hold down the fort from here while I run upstairs to get a better picture of what we're up against. How's that sound?"

"Like it's going to be harder for them to hit you than me."

The shooting coming from the street stopped, and James began backing away from the hotel's entrance and into the lobby. "Gotta move. I'll see if I can't distract our friends outside. That will be your cue to—"

"Give 'em a taste of their own medicine," Manning said. "Get going."

James streaked off, hurrying through the cramped hotel lobby and racing up the stairs past a terrified desk receptionist for the second floor. Manning, meanwhile, had to make sure the Iberian League attack force stayed put, otherwise the effectiveness of James's ploy would be wasted. The trick was to accomplish that task without getting his head blown off.

As an unnatural silence gripped the vicinity of the gun battle, Manning carefully advanced the few steps to the edge of the unprotected hotel entrance to look into the street. The kitchen smells of a nearby restaurant drifted his way, and the Canadian's stomach grumbled in response. Crouching and hugging the wall, the Phoenix Force specialist cautiously glanced a fraction of an inch around the corner of the doorway, instantly withdrawing to safety as a flurry of enemy bullets peppered the space his head had occupied. Assured that the Iberian League gunmen had not abandoned the scene, Manning maintained his firm grip on his Eagle .357 and settled down to wait for James to make his move.

Reaching the landing at the top of the second floor, James turned to the right and crossed to the door of one of the rooms facing the street. He tested the doorknob and found it locked. The door next to it was the same. Fresh gunfire filtered up the stairwell from downstairs.

"To hell with it," James said, planting his foot in a bone-jarring kick against the door, practically throwing it off its hinges.

Paying no attention to the nude prostitute and her customer huddling in fear on a sagging bed in the corner, James strode unceremoniously into the room and crossed straight to a window. Pulling back a dusty yellow curtain, he was presented with an unrestricted view of the street below. And not a second too soon, for even as the Stony Man crew's medic appeared at the window, four of the thugs were launching a full-scale assault on the hotel—specifically at the main entrance to the building where James had left Manning.

Tearing the curtain aside and lifting the window open in a rush of blinding speed, James leaned out and began firing his Colt at the killer leading the charge. Shot number one from the Colt grazed the advancing terrorist in the shoulder, and he staggered awkwardly to the left and fought to regain his balance. James corrected his aim, and this time the Commander's payload drilled a hot wet tunnel through the top of the gunman's skull. The doomed killer threw his hands into the air and tripped over his own feet, dead before his body could hit the street.

Spotting James at the window, the next assassin in line figured on an easy kill and raised his handgun to fire on the lanky American. The killer's intention progressed no further due to a Magnum-sized cavity of despair that mushroomed over his face as Manning rejoined the fight.

Two of the four IL terrorists were past tense. Another two remained, but in the cross fire of destruction following the deaths of their comrades, the final pair of gunmen discovered how easy it was to die. One hood went to his grave carrying a .45 caliber slug in his heart, while his partner in crime bowed out after making a futile bid to digest one of the Eagle's .357 eggs.

After the last of the attacking killers lost his life, James paused a moment to make sure no new bad-guys appeared out of the woodwork. When none did, the warrior from Chicago turned from the window and, after saying "Carry on" to the nude couple, hurriedly made his way out of the room and down-stairs to where Manning was waiting.

"All clear?" Manning asked.

"You got it," James confirmed. "Let's collect the runt I sapped with my Colt and hustle back to our car. Once the shock of the gunfight wears off, this neigh-borhood's going to be crawling with police."

"And it's better for us if they do their crawling alone," Manning said, exiting the hotel and hefting the unconscious IL terrorist onto his shoulder. "Where do you want to question this guy?"

"Someplace quiet."

15

The U.S. consul general wasn't overjoyed when his private fourth-floor office at Vía Layetana 33 was invaded by James and Manning, along with their bearded Iberian League prisoner. He was even less pleased when the Phoenix Force pros ordered him out of his own office so that they could conduct their investigation in total seclusion. Any formal refusal to comply with the order, however, was banished the moment James invited the consul general to telephone the White House if there was a problem with helping them out. Before the invitation to place the call was a minute old, Manning and James had the office all to themselves.

En route to their present location, the IL prisoner had partially regained consciousness. Now, as James propped the man up in a high-backed chair on rollers, the lone survivor of Barcelona's Iberian League terrorists opened his eyes and studied his unfamiliar surroundings with alarm.

"Where am I?" the terrorist demanded.

"That doesn't matter," James answered in Spanish. "All you need to know is that your planned attack against us failed. You've been taken prisoner and are now going to answer some questions."

The bearded killer leaned back confidently in the chair and smirked. "American fool, you are out of your mind. I will tell you nothing. My lips are sewn shut. Where are the rest of my friends?"

"Dead," James stated matter-of-factly.

The terrorist gulped audibly, and his brow grew damp with sweat. "Dead? All of them? What insanity are you telling me? Impossible! My friends cannot all be dead."

"Suit yourself," James said. "You are about to share their fate if you don't tell us about the Iberian League."

The terrorist's expression was smug. "Forget it. Whatever secrets I may or may not possess, the two of you will never know. Iberian League, you say? Never heard of it."

"We think otherwise," James countered, making a show of zipping open a black leather medical bag and removing a hypodermic syringe. "But that's okay." He held up the hypo. "Once we have a heavy dose of this burning through your veins, your memory is certain to improve." Grimly he advanced on the terrorist.

The man's bravado vanished as he squirmed as far back as he could in his seat. "What's the needle for?"

"To make you talk," James said. "In a few minutes you'll tell us everything we want to know, up to and including your mother's birthday, if that's what we want to find out." James stepped closer, holding the hypodermic syringe menacingly before him. "By the way, I hope your heart isn't weak."

The bearded killer nervously licked his lips. "What does my heart have to do with your questions?"

James held the hypo directly in front of the prisoner's face. "The drug in this syringe is very powerful. If your heart is strong, there won't be a problem. But if it's weak, well, I can't guarantee you will survive the interrogation."

James signaled to Manning, and the Canadian grabbed the assassin's arm in an ironclad grip. "Keep still," James commanded sternly, lowering the hypo to the captive's arm. "If I have to inject you with a second dose of this drug, you'll die for sure."

"Wait! Wait!" The terrorist thrashed on the chair like a fish out of water, his shaggy hair falling over his face. "There's no need to give me the drug. None! You want to know about the Iberian League? Fine. I will tell you, but without you pumping me full of whatever you have in the syringe."

James gave the terrorist a withering stare and didn't back away. "How can we possibly trust you? You will simply lie to save your own skin."

"No." The terrorist shook the hair away from his face. "I will tell you the truth. Anything. But you must promise not to inject me with the drug."

"A promise I can't make," James said. "Mind, if you are telling the truth, I'll be able to tell. I warn you that if I suspect you are lying, I will use the drug."

Manning said something in English, and James relayed the Canadian's comment to the prisoner. "My friend advises me to take no chances with you. He says you can't be trusted."

"But I can! I can! Give me the opportunity, and I'll show you. Test me. What do you want to know?"

"Tell us about the Iberian League," James instructed. "Were you and your friends flown into Barcelona from Madrid?"

"No. We were recruited locally several weeks ago by an Iberian League representative who lured us into the ranks with offers of easy money and the assurance that we'd be handsomely rewarded with additional riches if we joined. Practically all of us had criminal records and were unemployed at the time, so the offer to sign on was hard to refuse. Naturally, all of us were happy to accept."

"Who recruited you, what's his name?" James asked.

"He gave us a name, but we found out later it was false."

"That didn't disturb you?"

"Not really. The money he gave us was real enough, so there was no problem. Besides, the stranger said he was working for a man everyone knew of. With the amount of cash we were paid, this part of his tale was believable."

"And the name of the person supposedly employing the recruiter?"

"José Mantanez."

"Who is he?"

"Probably the biggest name in Spain's olive oil and wine business. Everyone knows of him. Señor Mantanez is a very wealthy man."

"And was it Mantanez or his recruiter who alerted you to expect us in Barcelona today?"

"Neither," the terrorist replied. "One of my friends you killed took the call, but told me afterward that the warning from Madrid had come from someone new. The caller didn't give his name."

"How many of you in Barcelona belonged to the Iberian League?"

"Counting me, there were a dozen of us."

"Including your dead friends and you that makes only eight," James said, gesturing with the hypo still in his hand. "I think you're lying to us."

"No! I speak the truth. There were twelve of us."

"What became of the other four members, then?"

"They were ordered to supplement the ranks of the Iberian League forces in Valencia—no doubt to assist in defeating the rest of your team. There are five of you altogether."

The terrorist sighed and scratched his beard. "We were told to expect your arrival, but were deceived as to your capabilities under fire. You aren't normal men or common soldiers. You fight like demons. If we had known, my friends and I might have done things differently. But we were deceived."

"One more question. The four men sent to Valencia," James began. "Where in Valencia were they getting together to launch their strike against the remaining three members of my team? Do you know?"

"It was nothing definite, only a possibility."

"Tell me, anyway," James ordered and, after the shaggy-haired terrorist obeyed the command, the commando from Chicago informed the IL killer in a tone laced with ice, "I should go ahead and use the drug on you, after all. Then I'll know without question you have told me the truth."

The prisoner reacted by struggling to evade the confines of his chair, but Manning's steely grip held him fast. "No! Not the needle. It isn't necessary. I told you the truth. You must believe me."

"For now." James stepped back. "But I warn you. If I discover later you have been lying through your teeth, we'll be back. And if I'm forced to return to settle with your lies, you've got my word you won't appreciate my second visit to Barcelona."

"I'm not lying," the terrorist insisted, convinced beyond doubt that James would like nothing more than to carry out his threat. "All I told you is true."

"We will be the judge of that," James said, then had Manning summon the consul general.

"He's all yours," Manning indicated the terrorist as the consul entered the office.

"What am I supposed to do with him?"

"Keep him under wraps for the next twenty-four hours," James said. "If you don't hear from us by then, you can turn him over to the Spanish authorities."

"But..." the consul started to protest.

"Unless, of course, you'd rather explain your objections to the White House?" James tapped his coat pocket. "I happen to have the telephone number handy right here."

The consul general lifted his palm as though he was halting traffic. "No. Leave the man here. This is all too fantastic."

"Thank you," Manning said. "Now we'd better be off. My partner and I have a plane to catch."

16

"Maybe I need a refresher course in Spanish," Encizo suggested. "Nothing I say seems to be getting through to these people."

McCarter pounded his fist into his hand. "Why don't you let me do the talking next time? Perhaps a little body English will succeed where simple Spanish has failed."

"We're going to have to come up with something," Katz said. "Somewhere in this city a gang of killers is poised to attack again. I'd hate to have them get away with more murder when we could have prevented it."

"We can't stop them if we can't find them," Encizo said. "We've been making the rounds now for more than two hours. How's our supply of pesetas holding out?"

"Just fine," McCarter answered. "We've got enough shekels in the kitty to line the pockets of Valencia's less savory characters from now until morning."

"And by then the Iberian League crazies will be ready to begin bumping off more tourists," Katz said. "I can't remember when I've felt so frustrated. My instinct tells me the IL hoods we're looking for are nearby, but at the rate we're tracking them down, they may as well be camped out on the dark side of the moon."

Encizo nudged McCarter as the three of them walked along. "Break open the bank. Here comes another customer."

As Manning and James had in Barcelona, Katz, Encizo and McCarter turned to the rougher sections of Valencia to try to drum up a viable lead on the Iberian League terrorists. Finding willing takers for the front money they were offering for information regarding their objective was easy. Indeed, at times during the incredibly sunny afternoon, everyone they met seemed to be looking for a handout. All their investment had netted so far, though, were sore feet and a dwindling bankroll—a major disappointment, considering the number of innocent lives riding on the outcome of their search.

Their latest "customer" stood bean-pole straight and wore his hair trimmed high over his protruding ears. His razor-thin mustache looked penciled in, and the eyebrows resembled a single furry caterpillar crawling over his forehead. He was dressed in loose-fitting baggy trousers and a silk-screened T-shirt bearing the face of Humphrey Bogart. Encased in sandals, his bare feet made flip-flopping noises as he walked. As soon as he saw the Stony Man trio approach, his crooked teeth flashed in a smile.

"There you are," he said in accented English. "I have been looking all over town for you."

"And why should you be doing that?" Katzenelenbogen asked the man.

"My name is Carlos Machado," the Spaniard introduced himself. "And the reason I have been looking for you is the same reason you have been looking for me. I am the answer to your prayers."

"And what have we been praying for?" the Israeli colonel questioned.

"Praying as well as paying, from what I hear," Machado corrected. "It is reported within certain social circles I am familiar with that you are seeking the persons responsible for murdering that poor German family earlier today. Is that not true?"

"We are busy men, Señor Machado," Katz answered. "What is it you have to tell us?"

"Better you should ask what it is I have to *sell* you."

"We're listening."

"Not so fast. First I must know what you are willing to pay for my information."

"That would depend entirely on the quality of your merchandise," Katz said. "What amount did you have in mind?"

Machado told him, and McCarter verbally entered the bargaining session. "This geezer's a right nutter. Give me a couple of minutes with him for a tender heart-to-heart, and I'll get him to bring his expectations down to earth."

Machado backed away from the Cockney. "Please, *señor*, I abhor violence."

"And I can't stand ruddy little twits like you who overprice themselves," McCarter said. "How much do you *really* want for this precious information of yours?"

"Perhaps you are right, *señor*," Machado told the Briton. "Perhaps my original figure was unreasonably high. Therefore, I am prepared to accept half of the fee I mentioned."

"Halve it once again, and you have yourself a deal," said Katz.

Machado beamed and held out his hand for the money. "Done."

The Israeli motioned to McCarter. "Pay the man...."

"*Gracias, señor.* Your bargaining skills are to be admired."

Katz ignored the compliment, then clarified his instruction to McCarter. "Pay him, but only half of the agreed amount."

McCarter nodded and began counting out the money as Machado protested to the Phoenix team's unit commander. "What trickery is this? I was under the impression we had a deal."

"And we do," Katz confirmed. "But I won't pay you in full for information that I haven't personally verified."

"I give you my word as a Spanish gentleman."

Katz shook his head. "Not good enough. You get half of your money as a down payment, and the rest when we know the true value of your merchandise."

"But," Machado objected, "the men you are seeking are extremely dangerous. Who is to pay me if the three of you are killed?"

"Admittedly, no one," Katz said. "But that is a risk you will have to take if we are to do business. Well?"

Machado took one look at the money clutched in McCarter's fist and made his decision, sweeping the wad of pesetas from the Briton's hand and stuffing the cash into a pocket of his baggy pants. "For somebody no longer so young, *señor*, you drive the hard bargain."

"Why don't we skip the poetry and get down to business?" Katz insisted. "What is it you have to tell us?"

"This, *señor*: the men you have come to Valencia to find are waiting to meet, greet and defeat you inside the bullring on the Calle Castellon. This they told me to relay to you should we have the opportunity to speak."

"And how is it they happened to single you out as their messenger?" Encizo spoke to Machado for the first time. "How do you explain that?"

"I cannot," Machado stated, his caterpillar eyebrows jumping on his forehead. "I only know what I know, and what I know is what they told me to tell you. Nothing more. Nothing less."

"These men who are waiting for us at the bullring?" Katz said. "How many of them did you see?"

"But two. They pulled up to the curb in their automobile as I strolled along the sidewalk, and called me over to their car. For a small fee—they were far less generous than you—they paid me to seek you out and deliver their message. This I have done, for Carlos Machado is an honest man."

"And the fact that you thought we'd be willing to pay for this message didn't hurt much either," Katz supposed.

"As I said," Machado repeated, "the men you seek were far less generous with their money than you. I see no harm in making a profit when and where I can. Living life at its fullest does not come cheaply. Why be satisfied with an appetizer when you can enjoy the whole meal?"

"Very well," Katz said. "Your point is well taken. But we hate to part company, and ask that you come along with us."

McCarter and Encizo flanked the Spaniard left and right as Machado asked suspiciously, "Where to?"

But all Katz said was, "Patience."

17

With their haggling informant, Carlos Machado, trussed up like a Christmas turkey in a single-bed hotel room, Katz, Encizo and McCarter proceeded to Valencia's bullring where the Iberian League killers were supposed to be waiting.

"Thar she blows," McCarter said as they reached their destination.

Encizo parked their rented car across the street from the bullring and read the marquee positioned over its main entrance.

"Ah-ha."

"What?" McCarter asked.

"Part of the bullring also serves as a museum," the Cuban answered.

The Briton shrugged. "Is that good or bad?"

"Good," Encizo said, watching a woman with two children in tow and carrying a bagful of souvenirs exit from the museum's doors. "The museum's open, and the bullring is closed. There's no bullfight scheduled for this afternoon."

"Excellent," Katz replied, getting out of the car while his companions did likewise. The three Phoenix Force commandos carried inconspicuous nylon gym bags containing the submachine gun each men favored. "If our friends from the Iberian League are inside the bullring, the absence of spectators will reduce the risk to innocent bystanders."

"Plus it will give us free rein to deal with the IL berks as we see fit," McCarter added.

"What's your guess on the best way for us to get inside?" Encizo asked Katz.

"That will be easy," the Israeli said with a laugh. "The tough part will come when we want back out again. Once the Iberian League has us where they want us, they're going to hit us with everything they've got."

"Fine by me," McCarter said impatiently. "The sooner the better."

Crossing the street after a break in the traffic appeared, the trio from Stony Man avoided the entry to the bullring's museum and began circling the structure on foot, searching for another way in. Within a minute they discovered a service entrance for concessionaires. The double doors had been conveniently left ajar.

"That was nice of them," McCarter said, getting to the service entrance first and, after checking to make sure the doors weren't booby-trapped, pulled them open. Once they were inside, the Briton quietly tugged the doors closed.

The Phoenix pros went to work immediately, unzipping their gym bags and removing their respective weapons—McCarter retrieving his Ingram MAC-10, Encizo, his H&K MP-5, and Katz, his dependable Uzi SMG. All of the subguns were outfitted with sound suppressors.

The section of the bullring they were in consisted of a long curving corridor running off to their right, while a shorter version of the hallway ran a short distance to the left before dead-ending at the rear of the bullring's museum. Directly across from where they stood were a pair of ramps, one climbing from the corridor they occupied to the spectator seats overhead, while the second led to a lower level of the bullring.

Although they listened carefully, the silence within the muted interior of the corridor gave no indication of the enemies' presence. A confined stillness filled the air. Nothing more. If the IL killers were stationed nearby, they were being damn quiet about it.

Katz motioned for the search of the bullring to begin, and McCarter indicated that he was willing to investigate the paved incline leading down. Encizo opted for the ramp going up, and Katz let it be known that he would continue following the corridor.

Katz tapped his left wrist with his hooked prosthesis, opened and closed his hand twice, then pointed to his feet: the Israeli colonel had nonverbally told his men to reunite at their present location in ten minutes' time. The other two nodded in understanding, then the three counterterrorists silently wished one another well and went their separate ways.

Keeping to the innermost wall of the corridor, Katz advanced like a lion on the hunt, noting with interest that each of the half-dozen doors he passed on his right was partially open, further proof that their opponents were expecting them. The Israeli kept walking, his senses alive, his Uzi at the ready.

Rafael Encizo reached the top of the ramp and found himself standing at the base of a short stone stairway. Sunlight illuminated the top of the stairs as he began to climb, his battle-forged instincts on the alert for the first sign of danger.

McCarter descended into semidarkness as he followed the ramp down into a world of cool dampness and earthy smells. At the base of the ramp was a dirt-floored copy of the corridor above. Countless footsteps had reduced the floor to a rock-hardness.

The Cockney paused and listened, thinking for a second he had heard something, but now it was gone. He licked his lips and swallowed, his throat dry, the urge for a Player's cigarette and a Coke coming and going in the same instant. He caressed the Ingram's trigger and stepped from the ramp, poised and eager to strike.

Twenty-five feet from the base of the ramp, McCarter came upon a doorway leading to an oblong room on his left. Further examination of the room revealed it to be some kind of holding pen for the animals used in the bullfights. The far wall of the room was obscured in darkness, while the solid wood door at its entrance was hanging wide open.

As he eased out of the deserted room, McCarter halted, his ears straining to detect anything out of the ordinary. He inhaled and exhaled slowly. The underground smells were growing stronger, a combination of anger and fear. Something else was there, too. A wild intangible so real that McCarter could taste it.

Oh, it's dying time again, the Londoner sang in his mind.

And he was right.

From out of the shadows of the curving tunnel ahead charged four Iberian League assassins on a mission of revenge, shrieking maniacally at the sight of their lone opponent. All of them were armed with submachine guns.

The terrorists' premature bout of overconfidence faded along with their ferocious grins as McCarter's noise-suppressed Ingram coughed to life, a third of the mighty MAC's magazine shredding the two terrorists in the lead to bloody ribbons. Perfectly disguised as instant corpses, the doomed duo collapsed onto the ground, and the IL pair left standing opened fire.

Acutely aware that he made a prime target, McCarter pivoted quickly and dived through the open doorway of the room behind him, barely clearing the entrance before a barrage of enemy lead from the corridor chewed away at the doorway. McCarter hit the ground, rolled out of his impromptu dive and bounced back onto his feet to confront his adversaries when the door swung shut with a crash and was latched from outside.

"Bugger all," the Briton muttered.

"We have you now," announced one of the IL gunmen in English from the opposite side of the door. "It is time to start speaking your prayers."

"Piss off!" McCarter called, sending a triple burst of Ingram rounds through the door.

"Ha!" laughed the terrorist, taunting the Englishman. "You will have to try harder than that."

Without wasting words or any more bullets, McCarter squinted in the darkness, attempting to gain a better view of his surroundings. But there wasn't much to see. A hundred shades of black, and that was it.

Moving so he was no longer in a direct line with the door, McCarter retrieved his cigarette lighter from his pocket and ignited it, causing flickering yellow shadows to dance about the room.

The walls and floor were bare. Beams of evergreen oak crisscrossed the ceiling. Against the back wall was the outline of another door, taller than McCarter, and its width twice the span of his shoulders. No doorknob or handle marred the door's smooth surface. McCarter snuffed out the flame and repocketed his lighter. For all intents and purposes, he was trapped.

"Hey!" the terrorist from the corridor shouted. "Are you still in there? Are you? Ha! Of course you are! But not for long."

The commando from London heard it then—the oversize door at the rear of the room sliding open. McCarter braced himself, expecting a hail of bullets to suddenly fill the room. What he got instead was the unmistakable sound of heavy breathing, and the stomping of hooves.

Not wanting to, yet unable to resist, McCarter again fished his lighter from his pocket, working his thumb over the striking wheel, holding down the gas lever to produce the brightest flame possible.

"Bloody hell!"

Framed in the doorway like a creature out of a nightmare was the largest, meanest-looking bull McCarter had ever seen. A thousand-pound engine of pure destruction with horns sharp as daggers, the bull's eyes were twin pools of red-reflected hate. The great beast snorted and lowered its head, its hooves stamping the ground anew, creating cracks upon the rock-hard floor.

"There's a good boy," McCarter said, keeping the flame of the lighter going, speaking as calmly as the situation dictated, and fighting back the urge to laugh out loud.

Right now his M-10 felt as useful as a squirt gun. He had no doubt of the Ingram's ability to bring the bull down, but with less than six yards separating him from the animal, it was not too difficult to picture himself being trampled to death before the bull decided to die.

"Hey!" the obnoxious voice of the terrorist teased. "How do you like your new friend? Eh?"

McCarter was mentally formulating an appropriate response to the terrorist's question when one of the hoodlum's companions, obviously the one responsible for the bull's entry into the room, fired a series of gunshots that came from behind the animal.

The bull snorted in rage, heaving its massive weight from side to side, then charged with a menacingly lowered head. In one swift motion, McCarter had turned and dropped his cigarette lighter to allow his Ingram to hang free by its lanyard. Darkness swallowed the room.

The Briton made a desperate dash straight for the door at the front of the holding pen, bent his knees and jumped upward, his hands scrambling blindly for the oak cross beams overhead. His fingers brushed against wood and held on, clawing for dear life, supporting McCarter's weight as he swung his legs forward, lifting himself out of the way as the rampaging bull swept by and below. The tips of the beast's horns tore the East-Ender's jacket.

The bull rammed the door, obliterating the wooden barrier in a crash of splinters and screams. The animal bellowed, and the screams grew louder. McCarter peered down from his elevated position through the shattered remains of the door as the two shocked Iberian League terrorists confronted the bull.

Goring one, then the other with its horns, the bull vented its fury on the assassins, bodily lifting the pair from the ground and tossing their bleeding, broken bodies into the air. In a matter of seconds it was over. The gunmen lay crumpled on the ground, and the bull vanished in a rush of pounding hooves.

Sensing movement behind him, McCarter let go of the cross beam and dropped to the floor, then spun around as the terrorist who had stampeded the bull prepared to attack. His subgun homing in on the Londoner, the IL hitman raced into the room, slipping and losing his footing after only three steps. The killer moaned, toppling forward, and McCarter helped him on his way with a double dose from the Ingram. Dual holes appeared on the Spaniard's chest, and he hit the dirt with a whoosh of exhaled air.

The dying gunman opened his eyes and sputtered in English as McCarter approached, "You are a very lucky man, *señor*. I almost killed you."

McCarter confirmed the cause of the terrorist's slippery fall, and told the killer just before he died, "Bullshit."

18

Katz had negotiated half of the bullring's ground-level corridor without incident when the muted sound of gunfire reached his ears. He turned and listened as the shooting stopped and started again.

Unsure whether the noise signaled trouble for McCarter or Encizo, Katz began sprinting back up the corridor, covering no more than a dozen yards before he learned he wasn't the only one to hear the shooting. That fact became evident after a door on his left slammed open, and four Iberian League gunmen who had been patrolling the perimeter of the bullring came pouring into the corridor.

The unexpected encounter almost surprised Katz as much as it did the IL squad. The key word, though, was "almost," for Katzenelenbogen's reaction time to the event left his opponents wondering what in the hell kind of hornet's nest they had stumbled into.

Training his Uzi on the killer in the lead, Katz cut loose with a 9 mm parabellum flurry that transformed the man's abdomen to a messy sieve. The enemy gunman screamed and doubled up, desperately grabbing the IL hood beside him to keep from falling—a dismal choice for help since this was the next Iberian League loser Katz targeted for destruction.

Unleashing a triple burst of capital punishment from his Uzi submachine gun, Katz saw his opponent give up the ghost and succumb to anonymity as most of the man's face was erased in a shower of blood. Trying to restore his identity, his nose hanging by a flap of skin, the gunman collapsed, taking down his still-shrieking partner nursing a bellyfull of lead.

With their original strength cut by half, the two remaining gunmen had no option but to continue their assault of the wild warrior they faced. Leaping over the bodies of their stricken comrades, the Spanish terrorists charged Katz from the left and right, triggering their SMGs.

Dropping below the intersecting line of enemy fire overhead, Katz disemboweled his nearest opponent with a hot blast from the Uzi, then corrected his aim to eliminate his final adversary. But the advancing gunman was too fast, jumping on Katz before he could shoot. A vicious kick planted in the Israeli's side sent his Uzi flying, skittering out of reach.

Deciding he would like nothing better than to stomp the one-armed troublemaker to death, the Iberian League killer lifted his booted foot to strike again, getting the shock of his corrupt life when the Israeli's three-pronged hooked prosthesis closed around his descending ankle. Fire shot up the terrorist's leg in a streak of white pain. Instinctively, he tried to pull back his foot, but that only made matters worse as Katz squeezed harder and refused to let go.

Through the cloud of agony engulfing him, the IL hood somehow remembered his weapon, his fevered mind concluding that using the Star Model Z-62 submachine gun was the only hope of saving his life. Katz had reached the same conclusion, however, and before the wounded gunman could implement his plan, the Israeli colonel released his hold on the enemy's ruined ankle in favor of clamping his prosthesis around the wrist of the hand clutching the Z-62.

Fresh fireworks of pain exploded along the length of the Iberian Leaguer's arm. His fingers flexed open, and gravity claimed his SMG. Lashing out, his free hand ineffectually struck Katz on the shoulder above his prosthesis. Katz ignored the feeble blow and increased the pressure of the steel hooks biting into his opponent's wrist.

Blood flowed in a pulsating river from the grisly wound. The killer lifted his free hand for another blow but froze midway through the attempt. His eyes tilted in their sockets, and consciousness drained from his system. The terrorist sagged, and the Israeli let him slide to the ground to sleep and bleed to death at the same time.

Katz recovered his Uzi and resumed his interrupted journey down the bullring's curving corridor. The clamor of gunfire in the distance was continuous now, and for the first time Katz could detect which direction it was coming from.

The unit commander of Phoenix Force put out a burst of speed. Unless he was mistaken, the Iberian League was using Encizo for target practice.

TWO IL GUNMEN GREW STIFF on the stone steps not far from Encizo, while another of the Spanish thugs had vanished from sight sucking air through a ventilated chest. But with at least five of the Iberian League savages still hell-bent on giving his illustrious career a permanent setback, Stony Man's Cuban representative found little reason to celebrate.

Sandwiched on his hands and knees between a long row of seats, Encizo couldn't fire his H&K MP-5 with any degree of accuracy without running the risk of a Spanish brand of lead poisoning. Concealed among the spectator seats located along the bullring's upper reaches, the terrorists had put their higher elevation to use by keeping Encizo pinned down and unable to move.

Encizo had been carrying out his investigation of the interior of the bullring when the first indication that IL forces were near made itself known in the form of gunshots from the vicinity of where he had split up with McCarter and Katz. The next shots he'd heard came from an entirely different source: a wave of Iberian League hoods attacked him from two directions at once.

Encizo met the assault with his customary skill and courage, aware of the odds against him but relentless in his determination to remain professional in the face of danger.

Delighting that they had cornered the Cuban on his own, the attacking terrorists' elation swiftly soured after Encizo showed them in a MP-5 kind of way how wrong they were to think him an easy kill.

The IL assassins were fast learners. After Encizo dusted off a pair of their frontline hotshots, then drilled a third man through the lungs, the terrorists appreciated the wisdom of rethinking their strategy. They did that while simultaneously firing upon Encizo, taking turns to race for the seats in the bleachers.

Encizo hugged the ground even more as the storm of bullets buzzing above his head threatened to part his hair, not at all reassured by the fact that the terrorists' aim was steadily improving. He crawled forward to see how good a bead the IL snipers had on him, and wasn't too surprised when the assorted slugs they were sending his way tracked his movement for every inch he gained. That disturbed Encizo, for it meant the terrorists could keep him locked into his present location, while they were free to safely realign their own position. When that happened, Encizo realized, the flimsy protection of the row of seats would be useless for cover.

"Oi!" McCarter's familiar voice shouted above the din of the IL gunshots, and the next minute his MAC-10 had entered the foray.

Immediately, the fusillade that had held Encizo in check ceased burning the air over his head. Instead, the terrorists were forced to concentrate all their attention on McCarter and his Ingram. Encizo looked up to witness his British friend catching one of the hoods in the open with a hail of M-10 discomfort before being chased by a barrage of gunfire behind and below a row of seats on Encizo's right.

The Iberian League's efforts to eliminate McCarter left one terrorist exposed to Encizo's MP-5 for several seconds, but that was more than enough time for Encizo to put his H&K machine pistol through its paces by tickling the ribs belonging to his IL target, one after another. The terrorist went rigid and allowed his weapon to slip from his fingers. Then he began swatting at the 9 mm hornets stinging his side. He was still beating away the pain eating at his rib cage when the spirit of life deserted him abruptly.

With McCarter's intervention and Encizo's return to active participation in the fight, the assassination team's overall strength had been reduced from five to three, a total that was certain to dwindle further as Yakov Katzenelenbogen came rushing onto the scene with his Uzi blazing. Appearing at the top of a stone stairway halfway up a cluster of seats to Encizo's left, the Israeli colonel gave the IL trio every reason to regret ever entering the Valencia bullring.

McCarter took his cue from Katz and came up shooting, and each of the Phoenix Force commandos knocked off one of their adversaries. The last gunman fell to the tune of Encizo's MP-5, toppling forward and bouncing down the bullring's steps with flailing arms and legs.

The three Phoenix soldiers waited to see if more IL gunmen would pop up, and when none did, reunited in the row of seats Encizo had been using for cover.

"Are you okay?" Katz asked Encizo.

The Cuban nodded. "Yeah, thanks. Good thing you guys came along when you did. Things were beginning to get pretty sticky."

"No matter," McCarter said, noting the numerous bodies decorating the interior of the bullring. "It looks like we got the lot of them."

"Before I was attacked I heard gunshots," Encizo said. "I take it the local Iberian League population wasn't limited to just these eight?"

"Right," Katz explained. "I found more of the terrorists on the other side of the bullring."

"So did I," McCarter confirmed. "Five of the twits tried sending me home in a box. Bad luck on their part, wouldn't you say?"

Before either Encizo or Katz could respond, their attention was diverted by the sound of running feet on the stone steps from the direction of their original entry into the bullring. Unsure whether additional IL forces were launching an attack, the three Phoenix pros spread out, ready to fill the entrance into the bullring with lead if need be, then relaxing a heartbeat afterward when Manning and James ran into view.

"Good timing," McCarter commented.

"Looks like you've been busy," James noted.

"We have," Encizo said.

"How was Barcelona?" asked Katz.

"About the same as here from the looks of things," Manning offered. "But we can tell you about that after we're out of here."

"What's the big rush?" McCarter wanted to know.

"*¡No se muevan!*" a bullhorn-amplified voice blared at them from the entrance that had just admitted James and Manning. "*¡Mantengan las manos visibles para mí!*"

Phoenix Force turned toward the voice and discovered an army of machine gun-wielding Spanish police looking down on them.

Katz nodded grimly and said to his men, "I think it would be a good idea if we didn't make any sudden moves."

McCarter laughed. "You've got my vote, guv."

19

Fernando Campos pounced on the ringing telephone like an owl going after a mouse. "Yes?"

"Hello."

Campos tensed. "Well?"

"The report isn't good. Things didn't go as we had hoped."

"In Barcelona or Valencia?"

"So far as your interests are concerned, both ventures ended disastrously."

"What?" Campos stammered. "Impossible! How could that be?"

"If we honestly knew the answer to that we wouldn't be discussing the matter, would we? The writing on the wall may not be a joy to read, but no amount of paint will gloss over the truth of its message."

"How extensive were our losses?"

"So far as I have been able to determine, total."

"One hundred percent? I can scarcely believe it. And the opposition? Given the nature of the reception committee we had waiting for them in each city, surely they must have suffered losses as well?"

"Not so you would know it. About their only setback to speak of is that all five have been placed under arrest by the police in Valencia."

"All five?" Campos was puzzled. "But I thought two of the troublemakers were in Barcelona."

"And so they were. But after they finished conducting business there, they flew to Valencia to help their friends."

"Well, at least that partly explains our poor showing in Valencia, then. If the five were reunited, our people were simply outclassed."

"More than you realize. The two from Barcelona didn't arrive in Valencia until after your entire reception committee there had been dealt with—by only three of the meddlers from America, not five."

"Wonderful. So where do we go from here?"

"How do you mean?"

"I'm surprised you'd need to ask. With all five of the bastards under arrest in Valencia, perhaps things aren't as grim as they seem."

"You can't expect the authorities in Valencia to hold the five indefinitely."

"Why not? They murdered Spanish citizens. How can the police turn a blind eye to that?"

"Easy. The five have friends in high places. Unless I'm mistaken, they will be released from custody and on their way back to Madrid within the hour."

"And there is nothing you can do to prevent it?"

"Nothing."

Campos sighed. "Hardly reassuring. You'll keep us posted as to further developments, of course?"

"Of course."

"Frankly," Campos said, "we expected your contribution to alleviating this deplorable situation to be much greater."

"I apologize if I have disappointed you, but mine is a delicate position. You and your colleagues must know I have done the best I could up until now."

"That may be," Campos said, "but from here on out, you will have to do better. So far, your best hasn't been good enough. Goodbye. We'll be waiting to hear from you."

"GOOD EVENING, COMISARIO DIAZ," Katz greeted as Manning opened the door and Diaz entered the room.

"And good evening to you," Diaz said. "It is good to discover my comrades in Valencia treated all of you well."

"We have no complaints," Katz said. "Thank you for joining us."

Diaz, attired in a Mario Borghetto single-breasted black-and-gray-striped suit, with a navy cotton check shirt and a Bianchini Ferier silk tie, arched his eyebrow. "What? And miss our hearing about your successful encounters with the Iberian League in Barcelona and Valencia? Never. It is all my men have talked about the entire afternoon. It is the prime topic of interest for every newscaster in the country.

"Naturally, Señor Feldman," Diaz addressed Katz by his cover identity, "neither you nor your associates are mentioned by name, description or photograph, but you can be sure the media are buzzing with the tale of how a mysterious group of unidentified individuals met with and vanquished the Iberian League terrorists today. In the hearts of Spain's citizens the five of you are being hailed as national heroes. You should feel justifiably proud."

Katz shrugged. "So long as the threat of the Iberian League is eradicated, who takes or is given credit for the deed isn't important. All that matters to us is that the terrorists are stopped. Which is why I am pleased you have joined us. We may have come across our first real break in the investigation."

"That is splendid," Diaz said. "Please elaborate."

Katz indicated Manning and James. "While Mr. Carson and Mr. Oliver were in Barcelona, not all the Iberian League terrorists they met up with were killed."

"Incredible," Diaz announced. "Clearly, there has been a communication breakdown somewhere along the line. I was not informed that any prisoners were taken."

"Prisoner," Katz corrected. "And there is nothing wrong with the flow of information within your department. Until this moment, we haven't revealed the fact that a prisoner was taken. Outside of the five of us, you are the first to know."

Diaz smiled. "Your confidence in sharing this with me is flattering, Señor Feldman."

"Not at all," Katz said. "We cannot expect to put this Iberian League problem to rest unless we work together. In the end we all want the same thing. Yes?"

"The end of the Iberian League, of course," Diaz said. "So, tell me more about this prisoner. Where is he now?"

"Safe," Katz returned, and Diaz left it at that. "And now that you are here, perhaps you could help shed some light on what the prisoner told us during questioning."

"What did you learn?" Diaz asked.

"While we were grilling him," James replied, "the prisoner didn't seem to know much about the man who recruited him and his pals into the Iberian League. He mentioned, in fact, that the name of the recruiter subsequently turned out to be false."

"Then how does that equate to a breakthrough in your investigation?" Diaz wanted to know.

"It doesn't," answered Manning. "But the name that the recruiter supplied to the prisoner to initially gain his confidence is another story. It is the name of the person who supposedly sent the recruiter to Barcelona in the first place."

"And who is this person?" Diaz asked.

"The prisoner told us it was a man named José Mantanez," James said.

Diaz laughed out loud. "José Mantanez? Forgive me, *señor*, but what you suggest is preposterous. Considering the source of this fantasy, however, and the conditions under which it was formed, I can say without hesitation that the prisoner's accusation is absolutely untrue. Evidently, what with his fellow terrorists having been killed, the man you questioned concocted the wildest lie he could imagine in order to have something to say. It was probably the first thing that popped into his corrupt little mind."

"How can you be so sure?" McCarter asked.

"Easy," Diaz said. "Señor Mantanez is one of Spain's wealthiest and most respected citizens. It is ludicrous to assume that a gentleman of Señor Mantanez's stature would involve himself in terrorist atrocities attributed to the Iberian League. It is unheard of."

"I disagree," Encizo countered in a tone laced with doubt. "Isn't it true that José Mantanez's fortune is built upon the wealth he reaps from his olive oil and wine concerns?"

"What of it?" Diaz asked. "The connection between olive oil and wine and the Iberian League murderers escapes me. It hardly implicates Señor Mantanez. What could he possibly hope to gain by becoming involved in such madness?"

"That's easier to figure out after you tie Mantanez in with what we discovered during our research at the library," Encizo was quick to reply. "Primarily, Spain's membership in the EEC means that many of your country's businesses will be matching their manufactured products against foreign competitors like never before. The financial impact of this competition is expected to affect everyone, especially people such as Señor Mantanez who, until now, enjoyed unrestricted control over a particular domestic market."

"So the wine Señor Mantanez sells will have to compete with wine from France and Italy," Diaz said. "You will have to forgive me, but I will need proof stronger than that before I am ready to hang the man."

"And so will we," Katz agreed. "That is why we have shared this information regarding José Manta-

nez with you. If we are wrong about Señor Mantanez, then we want to know. If, on the other hand, he
is involved with the Iberian League, we want to know
that, too.''

''I will do everything within my power to see that
Señor Mantanez's good name is cleared,'' Diaz
promised. ''To accomplish that goal, how may I be of
assistance?''

''By helping us locate Señor Mantanez so that we
may question him,'' Katz said. ''Will finding him be
difficult?''

''Not very,'' Diaz decided. ''It is well known that he
has an estate in Córdoba that he frequents. Still, to
save time wasted on an unnecessary journey, I had
better determine Señor Mantanez's whereabouts
through sources at my disposal.''

''That would be excellent,'' Katz confirmed. ''How
much time are we talking about?''

Diaz thought a moment. ''An hour or two at the
most. My contacts are very thorough.''

''Until we hear from you, then.'' The Israeli extended his left hand. ''Thank you for your assistance,
Comisario Diaz. It is much appreciated.''

Diaz shook Katz's hand. ''I do what I do, Señor
Feldman.''

''I have to admit,'' Manning commented once Diaz
was gone, ''that the *comisario*'s new spirit of cooperation is refreshing after all the crap he dished out to
us when we first arrived in Spain.''

''Maybe he has more reason to cooperate now than
before,'' speculated Katz.

''How do you figure?'' James asked.

"Nothing carved in stone, mind you," Katz said, "but you would think, given our assurance to Diaz that we would keep him apprised of our actions, that he would have expressed some annoyance at not being told we were going to Valencia and Barcelona."

"You've got a point," Encizo said. "Taking into account his past behavior, Diaz should have been pissed off we slipped out of town without telling him."

"And yet," Katz added, "Diaz didn't so much as mention it."

"You can't knock the results we've chalked up so far," Manning said. "Perhaps one of Diaz's superiors put salt on his tail and got him to get off our case."

"Anything is possible," Katz said. "One thing for sure, though, is that someone has been tripping up our investigation since we first hit Spain."

"And you think it might be Diaz?" James asked.

"I don't know," Katz told his partner from Chicago. "It's just something in the back of my mind I thought I'd share. In any event, I don't think it will hurt to keep Diaz under closer observation from here on out."

"Right," McCarter said. "If our Spanish fashion plate isn't all he's cracked up to be, we don't want to be the last to know."

20

"Really, José," Fernando Campos said, referring to the oversize tumbler his Iberian League partner had filled with Scotch and cola. "Aren't we being a trifle premature?"

"Not on your life," Mantanez shot back, his bald head slick with sweat as he tilted the tumbler to his lips and downed a third of his drink. "Something else has gone wrong. I can feel it in my bones."

Eduardo Vera demanded, "What is all this talk, José? Just because our contact telephoned to request a meeting with us, you are more than ready to go off the deep end."

"It wasn't just any meeting he requested," Mantanez corrected, feeling somewhat calmer now that the liquor was beginning to surge through his system. "But an 'emergency' meeting." He looked at Campos. "That is what he said, isn't it?"

"I won't deny it," Campos said. "But 'emergency' could mean anything. For all we know, our contact is coming to tell us that the team of investigators from America have called it quits and are returning to the United States."

"You had better pinch yourself on the ass, Fernando," Mantanez advised, "because you are dreaming. Our five headaches from Washington are not about to go home with their job half-finished, and you damn well know it.''

Mantanez guzzled more of his drink, then went on, ''Have you two taken a good look recently at what has become of our Iberian League troop strength since those five maniacs came to Spain? Have you? We're not fighting to get Spain to withdraw from the EEC anymore; we're too busy feeding Spanish cemeteries.''

''No one ever pretended it was going to be easy,'' Vera cautioned.

''True,'' agreed Mantanez. ''Yet no one ever guessed it was going to be this kind of nightmare, either. Our people are being slaughtered faster than we can replace them. Do you know what that means? At the rate we're going, there won't be anyone left but us three, and if it comes to that, what we envisioned when we created the Iberian League will perish forever. And you know why? Because those five bastards from the U.S. will track us down and murder us.''

''I'm afraid you're blowing the situation totally out of proportion,'' Campos said. ''I agree we've been losing men at an alarming rate but, as we decided, with our nation's unemployment rate habitually in the clouds, we won't have an enduring problem enticing new members to join our ranks.''

''No?'' Mantanez said, smirking as he upended his glass and drained the tumbler dry. ''You're talking about yesterday, Fernando. You're talking about when we could point out to the new recruits the advantages of Iberian League membership. What do we tell them now...if they're dull-witted and stupid and especially eager to die, then sign on the dotted line? Ridiculous! Talk sense.''

Mantanez, who had been hovering near the bar, moved behind it to prepare himself another drink.

''I wish you would delay having a refill, José,'' Campos said. ''I would like to present to our contact a picture of unity and resolve, and we can hardly expect that with you slurring your words and sweating like a pig. Show a little backbone without getting it out of a bottle for a change!''

Now Mantanez turned on Campos. ''Idiot! Just because you are too damn ignorant to comprehend the crisis we are in, don't go taking it out on me!''

''Gentlemen! Gentlemen!'' Vera intervened. ''Please. Enough of this harsh exchange of words. I'm sure it would give our enemies immense satisfaction to know how agitated we have become. Let's put an end to it, I say.''

Campos relaxed and took a seat. ''Of course, you are right, Eduardo,'' he told Vera. ''It is senseless for us to be shouting at one another when we are supposed to be friends.'' He smiled at Mantanez and held out his hands in a gesture of peace. ''José, can you see the wisdom of Eduardo's counsel? The three of us are friends, good friends, and we mustn't allow ourselves to behave otherwise. Can you ever forgive me for speaking so harshly to you?''

''I've already put the matter out of my mind,'' Mantanez said politely.

Campos smiled. "I'm glad to hear that. Pay no attention to my earlier outburst. If you would like another drink, please feel free to help yourself."

"Thank you," Mantanez said, "but no. Upon reflecting on what you told me, albeit in anger, I find a germ of truth. My nerves may be on edge, but drinking myself into a stupor is not the solution to calming them." He set the empty tumbler down and stepped away from the bar. "My thirst for Scotch and cola has deserted me."

A firm knock sounded on the door.

"Ah," Campos noted, "that will be our contact now. I left word that he be sent upstairs as soon as he arrived." Campos settled back into his chair and called out in a loud clear voice, "Enter."

The door opened, and Comisario Diaz stepped into the room, silently acknowledging each of them before speaking directly to Campos. "I don't have that much time, so we will have to make this brief."

"We're listening," Campos said. "You asked for an emergency meeting, and we are here. What is it you have to tell us?"

"I just came from the Hotel Plaza where the investigative team from America is staying," Diaz said. "I'm saddened to report that today's disasters in Barcelona and Valencia must be measured by more than mere loss of Iberian League soldiers. The toll runs higher than that."

"Go on," Campos urged reluctantly, anxious for whatever bad news Diaz brought with him to come out into the open. "We didn't think you called this meeting simply to hear yourself talk. What else?"

"When I spoke to you earlier, Señor Campos," Diaz said, "I was under the impression that none of your people survived the Valencia/Barcelona encounters."

"And now?" Eduardo Vera inquired.

"Now I know that one of your men in Barcelona wasn't killed. He lived through the battle with two of our adversaries, and was summarily questioned by them. Although the background information he could supply was sketchy at best, he provided his captors with a name. That name was José Mantanez."

"What!" Mantanez fairly screamed out the word. "Do you mean to say an Iberian League soldier taken prisoner actually gave my name to our enemies?"

"Precisely," Diaz confirmed.

"What did they do?" Campos asked. "Torture our soldier to give out the name?"

"I don't know," Diaz said. "However they came to have Señor Mantanez's name, though, they seemed pretty certain that its connection to the Iberian League was authentic. They don't know how, but they are convinced Señor Mantanez is involved with the Iberian League in some capacity."

"Well, that is wonderful, isn't it?" Mantanez snapped. "Some cowardly bastard on our payroll lets my name slip, and now my head is on the chopping block!"

"Hold on," Campos said, giving Mantanez's tirade a rest. "Tell us—" he nodded at Diaz "—now that our foes possess one of our names, what do they intend to do with it?"

"When I last saw them they were finalizing their plans for apprehending Señor Mantanez and bringing him in for questioning."

"Mother of God," Mantanez moaned. "What nightmare is this? My worst fears realized!"

"What is to be your role in this proposed apprehension?" Campos asked Diaz, wishing Mantanez would settle down and quit acting like a buffoon. "What are they expecting of you?"

"No more than before," Diaz began, only to have Mantanez interrupt.

"When they told you their Iberian League prisoner had divulged my name, what was your response?"

"That the prisoner's accusations were preposterous and had no basis in fact. I explained that Señor Mantanez is one of Spain's most respected citizens and businessmen, and that it was desperate fabrication on the part of their informant to link Señor Mantanez to the Iberian League. I said everything I could think of to throw them off the trail."

"And?" Mantanez said the word as though it was being squeezed from a winepress as Diaz lifted his shoulders in an eloquent shrug.

"The five men questioning me would hear none of it. They have it in their minds to speak to Señor Mantanez, and will not be satisfied until they do."

"How do they propose to locate him?" Vera wondered.

"Through my assistance," Diaz said. "When they inquired how difficult it would be to find Señor Mantanez, I replied, not very, and was obliged to tell them about his estate in Córdoba."

Mantanez cut loose with a giddy laugh. "I must be going deaf." He glanced in anger at Vera and Campos. "Did I hear this son of a bitch correctly? He voluntarily informed them of my Cordoban estate?"

"One doesn't play guessing games when sitting before lions," Diaz offered in his defense. "Besides, I told them nothing they couldn't learn by asking practically anyone. And if someone supplied information to them after I feigned ignorance on the subject, then it wouldn't go well for me. My cover would be blown."

Campos said to Mantanez, "What Comisario Diaz says is true, José. If he hadn't faithfully answered our enemies' questions, then their suspicions would have been aroused, and we could have lost our sole contact within the Madrid police. We've gained much from our association with the *comisario*; let's not undervalue that relationship now."

"That's easy for you to say, Fernando," Mantanez scoffed. "After all, it's not you the five investigators are looking for. It's easy for you to sit comfortably when it's my ass that's over the fire."

"If I may interject?" Diaz said. "While Señor Mantanez has every right to be upset, I do believe he is jumping the gun. Merely because the five know of the estate in Córdoba doesn't mean they have to find Señor Mantanez there."

"What bright idea now?" Mantanez complained. "Am I to go into hiding like some common criminal off the streets?"

"That's not what I am suggesting, either," Diaz said.

"I don't know why we're even discussing it," Mantanez fumed. "We know the five seeking to destroy us are all presently at the Hotel Plaza. They are gift-wrapped and waiting for us. Then why not hit them there with everything we've got? Level the place if we have to, but make sure our enemies don't leave the hotel alive."

"Out of the question," Vera decided, without having to think about it. "We have already tried disposing of our five opponents, a venture that proved far from successful. The futility of launching a similar attack, even on a grander scale, has little merit so far as sound strategy is concerned.

"Even if we were able to smuggle enough of our soldiers into the Hotel Plaza unnoticed, and they somehow managed to kill the five investigators, there is no guarantee our men could leave the hotel without having to battle their way through a barricade of Madrid police."

"Which," Diaz offered, "is easy to imagine happening. The recent activities of the Iberian League has everyone connected with Spanish law enforcement dancing on a skillet, constantly on the alert for a way to publicly engineer a strike against the Iberian League. Remember, the five men from the United States are the only ones who directly confronted the so-called terrorists—a source of embarrassment to virtually everyone associated with the law. No, you can trust and believe that the Cuerpo General de Policía and the Policía Armada would like nothing more than to trap the Iberian League soldiers inside the Hotel Plaza.

"And don't think that if such an event occurred your forces could purchase their freedom using hostages. If the authorities were convinced they could contain a major number of Iberian League gunmen, then they would naturally, under the circumstances, expect civilian casualties."

"And if some of our men managed to escape," Campos added, "the damage to the Iberian League's credibility would be irreparable. So, I'm sorry, José, but I must side with Eduardo. Hitting our foes while they remain at the hotel is out."

"Well, something has to be done," insisted Mantanez. "*I* must do something. Those five bastards are looking to tan my hide and tack it to the wall."

Eduardo Vera pointed a finger at Diaz. "You were saying, *comisario*, that you didn't recommend having our enemies journey to Córdoba in search of Señor Mantanez?"

"That is correct," Diaz said, "for their doing so would eventually draw the wrong kind of attention to Señor Mantanez—something to avoid at all costs."

"Agreed," Vera said.

"Keeping the spotlight off Señor Mantanez is even more important," Diaz added, "because the five investigators have told no one except me about the connection they have made between Señor Mantanez and the Iberian League."

"And you believe this?" Campos asked.

"Yes," Diaz said. "They are a secretive lot. They informed me of their prisoner's confession only because they are certain of my loyalty. I am, after all, a lieutenant colonel on the police force."

"All right," Mantanez said, "so we won't send those gangsters from America to my estate in Córdoba. No matter how well we fortify the estate, there is no reason to lure our enemies there if it will serve to besmirch my good name. Better still to concoct a scheme whereby they take the secret of my Iberian League association with them to their graves."

"Which is what I intend to propose," Diaz said. "If we can entice the five in question to a location of our choosing, then the Iberian League should be in the enviable position of silencing them forever."

"Yes," Campos said, "and I believe I know the perfect place for the job."

Campos presented his choice, and there were no dissenters. Even José Mantanez found himself accepting the location without protest. What Mantanez *did* object to, though, was Campos's and Vera's insistence that he travel to the site to oversee the expected confrontation.

"You know as well as we do, José," Campos said, "that the men will be more apt to fight for the Iberian League's cause with you there to lead them. It's past the time when an armchair commander will suffice. One of us should be calling the shots and, seeing as how your name is the one our enemies possess, it's only fair you should be the one to go."

Numb with the decision made by his partners, Mantanez remained silent while Campos and Vera hammered out additional details with Diaz. As soon as Diaz was gone, Mantanez headed straight for the bar and filled his tumbler with all the Scotch and cola the oversize glass could hold.

Neither Campos nor Vera remarked on Mantanez's flight to the bottle. With what their baldheaded compatriot had facing him, they figured he could use all the help he could get.

DIAZ RETURNED to the Hotel Plaza less than two hours after his initial departure.

"That was fast," Katzenelenbogen remarked once Diaz had entered the suite. "We really weren't expecting you back so soon."

"Not at all, Señor Feldman," Diaz said. "With the substantial resources available to me in my capacity as *comisario* of the Cuerpo General de Policía, learning the whereabouts of a man such as José Mantanez is strictly standard procedure."

"You discovered where we can locate Señor Mantanez?" Katz asked.

Diaz nodded. "Of course. And it's a good thing that I checked, for it turns out that Señor Mantanez is, indeed, not presently at his estate in Córdoba."

"Where do we find him, then?" Manning quizzed.

"Señor Mantanez is currently paying a visit to his nephew in Seville," Diaz replied, tapping his breast pocket. "I have the address, so the nephew's residence shouldn't be that difficult for you to find." He started to withdraw the address from his pocket, but Katz stopped him.

"Giving us the address won't be necessary," the Israeli explained. "If you don't mind, we would like it if you accompanied us to Seville to help apprehend Señor Mantanez."

"Go with you to Seville?" Diaz repeated, as though he hadn't understood. "You want me to accompany you?"

"Yes," Katz answered. "You need time to change into something more appropriate, of course, but we'd like to depart for Seville within the hour."

"Certainly, I am flattered at your request," Diaz said, "but unfortunately, on such short notice, traveling with you personally to Seville is impossible. As you are aware, I am conducting my own investigation into the Iberian League's affairs, and my presence would be sorely missed. Please accept my heartfelt apologies."

The suite's telephone rang and Encizo answered it, then passed the receiver to Diaz. "It's for you."

Diaz smiled and took the call, muttering no more than three or four syllables during the entire conversation, then said goodbye and returned the telephone to Encizo's outstretched hand. "It appears my investigation has been put on temporary hold," Diaz announced with suspicion, "and I've been ordered to remain on duty as your personal assistant for so long as you deem necessary. I will, it seems, be going with you to Seville after all."

"How about that?" Katz grinned. "What perfect timing."

"Speaking of which," James said, "we'd better move."

"This nephew of Mantanez's," Katz said. "What does he do in Seville?"

"He owns a chain of hairdressing salons," Diaz answered. "He is what you would call a very wealthy barber."

McCarter laughed. "Bloody well figures, doesn't it?"

21

"It's almost midnight," the man said.

"Am I such a fool that you don't think me capable of telling time?" José Mantanez barked at his subordinate. "I know it's close to twelve o'clock. What of it?"

"I merely mentioned the time in passing," the Iberian League soldier answered. "I meant to imply nothing derogatory. If I offended you, Señor Mantanez, it wasn't my intention."

"Yes, well, perhaps I reacted a bit hastily," Mantanez said, already feeling like a fool. "It's not as though we haven't been under an extraordinary amount of hostile pressure these past few days."

"No sir. Hopefully, with any luck, Señor Mantanez, we will be the cause for relieving the pressure that has backed us into a corner. If the American marauders do attack us this evening, then I think they will discover their recent string of successes has come to an abrupt end.

"Confidentially, most of us feel our losses to date resulted from a lack of confidence and resolve on the part of our fallen comrades to drive the five Washington devils from our shores. You may rest assured, Señor Mantanez, that the men guarding this Seville villa are true patriots of Spain. None of us lack the conviction required to defeat our enemies should they mount a strike against us."

"Oh, they will be here, my friend," Mantanez promised, grateful that the toes curling with dread inside his shoes couldn't be seen. "Of that you may be sure. And when they do arrive, I will be staking my life, as well as the future of the Iberian League, upon you and your men to embrace their challenge with courage befitting a native son of Spain."

"And it will be a challenge well met," the Iberian League soldier vowed, then excused himself to continue making his security-check rounds of the villa.

Mantanez watched the young terrorist go and breathed a welcome sigh of relief. So full of alcohol that he could barely stand, Mantanez crossed on unsteady legs to the third-story room he was using as a command center. Once he was inside, he closed the door behind him and sought the nearest chair, a high-backed cushiony effort whose flamboyant upholstery made him wince.

Campos and Vera had cooked his ass for sure, but what was he to do? Run? Even if he could manage to slip away undetected, where would he go? He was a public figure who was well-known to the media. Once it became known that the police were searching for him, there would be no place he could hide.

So he sat in a room in Seville, drunk and afraid, waiting for the five American madmen to show up, and doing his best not to flood the floor with the ocean of Scotch and cola floating in his gut. He belched, and something greasy and sour jumped to the back of his throat. He swallowed, and the horribly bitter taste disappeared.

Although the plan formulated by Fernando Campos called for use of the villa where Mantanez's nephew supposedly lived, no nephew of José's resided there at all.

Actually, the villa was owned and maintained by Campos as an occasional vacation hideaway for him and close friends. Campos traditionally used the villa when he wanted to get away from it all, and to ensure his privacy he always entered and left its premises under the cover of darkness.

Because the villa had been purchased under an alias, Campos had reasoned, and Vera agreed, that Seville was the best place in Spain to lure the five troublemakers to their doom. And if the authorities were to conduct an investigation into the matter after the team from the States was eliminated, nothing they would uncover would steer them in the direction of the Iberian League's three bosses.

So Mantanez sat and waited, contemplating his grim prospects for the future, feeling very much the condemned man. Campos and Vera had most definitely dumped his ass in a stew, and already the heat was too much for him to bear.

CROSSING THE BRIDGE over the Río Guadalquivir, Phoenix Force along with Diaz, headed for the Barrio de Triana, one of Seville's picturesque quarters.

With Gary Manning handling the driving chores of the unmarked police van Diaz had secured at Seville's airport, the six men completed the final leg of their journey in silent contemplation: Phoenix Force wondering whether another clash with the Iberian League was in the offing, while the pensive Diaz pondered how best to extricate himself from his deplorable situation in one piece.

Diaz didn't doubt for a second that the one-armed fox calling himself Feldman pulled strings to get him reassigned from his duties in Madrid to coerce him to go along with whatever mad scheme they had in store. And Diaz was helpless to do anything about it. To raise a stink at this stage of the game would be suicide. Many Iberian League soldiers had died because of these five, and Diaz was in no great hurry to personally contribute to their number. If Feldman and his four friends learned he had been working against them from the start, Diaz felt in his heart he would never live to celebrate his thirty-sixth birthday.

For his part, Yakov Katzenelenbogen was still awaiting the jury's verdict on Diaz. After he was reassigned to fly with Phoenix Force to Seville, the *comisario* had abandoned the footdragging he had displayed previously and made a big show of doing everything he could to make their journey to Seville a successful one.

In addition to the van they were riding in, Diaz had acquired a set of glossy photographs featuring their primary objective in Seville, José Mantanez. The photos would permit Phoenix Force to pick Mantanez out of a crowd, a feat they hoped to pull off with Mantanez alive and kicking.

"Turn **left** here," Diaz instructed, referring with a penlight to the hand-drawn map he removed from his pocket.

Manning followed the police lieutenant colonel's directions, and sent their van around a corner and up a street lined with residences on either side. "How much farther?" the Canadian asked.

"Less than a kilometer, I believe," Diaz answered, again checking his map. "I will let you know."

Katz paid attention as Diaz spoke, listening carefully for any inflection of betrayal in the Spaniard's voice. Though he could detect an undercurrent of nervousness in the *comisario*'s words, the Israeli realized the basis for this could easily be their mission in Seville. Every soldier reacts differently to a combat situation and, for all Katz knew, the strain he detected was simply tension born out of Diaz's coping with the unknown.

Rather than give Diaz the benefit of the doubt, however, Katz preferred to keep close tabs on the man until he could be sure of his true colors one way or the other. While this put the burden of proving his loyalty on Diaz, it also prevented Katz, or the men under his command, from lowering their guard in the company of a potential enemy.

"All right," Diaz said. "Park anywhere you want along here, and we will go the rest of the way by foot."

"You got it," Manning said, bringing their van to a halt at the first available spot he could find. He killed the headlights, did the same to the van's engine, then turned in his seat. "End of the ride, guys."

"And about time, too," McCarter announced, opening the vehicle's door and climbing outside. "No names mentioned, mind you, but some of us sit behind the wheel like they were pushing a bleedin' pram."

"No names mentioned," Manning shot back, "but it sure beats the roller-coaster approach to driving."

The rest of Phoenix Force, and Diaz, followed McCarter's example and emerged from the van into Seville's cool night air. At the far end of their street the amber taillight of a single automobile signaled for a turn, then was gone, leaving the six intruders alone on the avenue.

Katz and company had come to Seville hoping to apprehend and take José Mantanez into custody with a minimum of aggravation—courtesy of a soft probe of the wine merchant's nephew's home. That way they could be in and out and on their way without waking half the neighborhood.

Soft probes, though, had notoriously poor reputations for turning hard when least desired. Accordingly, Phoenix Force had attired and armed themselves to expect the worse.

Even Diaz seemed to be taking the thought of a possible fight seriously, having discarded his usual fashionable threads in favor of battle fatigues, in addition to arming himself with an autopistol and submachine gun, both weapons chambered for 9 mm rounds.

"If my map is correct," Diaz said, speaking in a whisper, "the villa of Señor Mantanez's nephew is a short walk up the street at number 668. At this late hour it is unlikely the gates of the villa will be open, so we will either have to risk triggering some kind of security alarm by climbing over the wall surrounding the villa, or we can attempt to force the gate open to gain entry.''

"If Uncle Mantanez is visiting his nephew on his own," McCarter said, "and there are no Iberian League heavies camped on the nephew's doorstep, then there's a third option we might consider, namely having one of us ring the bell at the front gate and ask to be let in. Unfortunately, my way requires someone who speaks Spanish.''

"I don't believe it," Manning told the Cockney. "Since the only other language I speak is German, that's the first scheme in memory you've come up with that doesn't have my name written all over it.''

The British commando smiled. "Give me a tick, and I'll think up another one, then.''

"Why don't I ring the bell?" Encizo volunteered, glancing at Katz. "How's that sound?''

"Like sweet sensible music," the team's unit commander replied. "If we can get in without conquering the wall, so much the better. Going through the gate offers the path of least resistance. We'll position ourselves on either side of the gate before you do and take it from there.''

"So, let's do it," Encizo said. "Let's see if anybody's home.''

Taking the lead, the Cuban warrior noiselessly set off down the street, with his five companions following close behind. As it was unlikely anyone would open the gate for him while he was obviously heavily armed, Encizo readjusted his weapons, primarily his H&K MP-5 machine pistol, so it was hanging out of sight but within easy reach beneath his coat.

Encizo slowed as he approached the address they were looking for, his mind keenly alert for any indication of Iberian League sentries lurking about. But the nearer he drew to the gate—a solid wood eight-foot-high barrier with a door in one side—the more evident it became that the area directly in front of it wasn't guarded.

Encizo gave the others the all-clear sign, then waited while they moved into position, with McCarter, Katz and Diaz going to the left of the gate, Calvin James and Gary Manning taking up a stance on the right.

Encizo stood back from the gate to study the villa on the opposite side. Only the building's top two floors were visible, appearing pale and white against the background of the night. All the second-story windows were shielded by ornate metal bars, while a small balcony outside one of the third-floor rooms watched over the villa's courtyard below. Save for the glow of an electric light from the balcony room, the villa was swathed in darkness.

Satisfied there was nothing else worth seeing, Encizo crossed straight to the door in the gate and gave a hearty pull to a narrow length of rope sticking through an opening. Immediately, from within the villa itself, the musical chimes of an unfamiliar song were heard. When the chimes ceased to play, the Cuban tugged on the bellpull once more, and the tune was repeated inside the villa.

Presently, there came the sound of shuffling steps along the villa's courtyard, heading toward the gate. The shuffling feet stopped at the gate, and an eye-level security window fixed into the door was opened.

"Who comes calling at this late hour?" an irate voice demanded through the tiny window. "Virtually everyone in the villa is asleep, which is what I was doing before you disturbed me. What is it you want?"

"I regret the intrusion," Encizo apologized, "but I bring an urgent message that must be delivered to Señor Mantanez."

"Oh?" the male voice said through the opening in the door. "And what message is so important that it can't wait until morning?"

"There was an accident at Señor Mantanez's estate in Córdoba," Encizo replied, thinking fast. "Certain damage was inflicted to the premises, the specific details of which I was instructed to relay to Señor Mantanez in person. Has he retired for the evening?"

"No, he hasn't, but..."

"Then I insist you let me in," Encizo said. "Don't delay. Señor Mantanez is sure to want the news I bring, and he will be most angry if you make him wait until morning. Open the door and let me in."

"Oh, very well."

The security window was closed, and the door mounted in the gate swung open, revealing a man several years younger than Encizo. The man wore a plain cotton shirt, trousers and leather sandals. He moved aside and motioned for the Cuban to enter.

"But try not to wake the rest of the household," the man said. "You may not need your sleep, but some of us do."

"Don't worry." Encizo stepped through the doorway to the courtyard. "I will deliver my message and be gone before you know it."

Encizo started walking toward the villa when the man called out, "Hold on while I relock the door."

As he turned to do so, Encizo threw open his coat and brought out his MP-5. "That won't be necessary."

"What?" The man spun away from the gate, his eyes riveted on Encizo's gun as he automatically raised his hands into the air. "I don't understand."

"You don't have to," Encizo told him. "Just do as I say, and you won't be harmed."

The door swung open again, permitting Katz and the others to come in. Manning was the last to enter, and he shut the door behind him.

"Now what?" Encizo's prisoner asked without commenting on the latest arrivals. "What do you want?"

"The same as before," Encizo said. "To speak with Señor Mantanez. Is that his room on the third floor?"

"Yes."

"Good. You will take us there now. And don't try anything foolish. I'd hate to have to shoot you, but won't hesitate if you give me sufficient cause."

"You have nothing to fear from me, *señor*," the Spaniard said, "for I am unarmed and don't wish to die."

"This is welcome news for both of us," Encizo said. "Now move."

With his hands reaching for the sky, the Spaniard obeyed the command.

22

They were almost across the courtyard when the villa's front door burst open, and a half-dozen Iberian League gunmen stormed outside.

"Die!" hissed the sandaled terrorist covered by Encizo.

The six IL killers began firing an instant later, but Phoenix Force and Diaz had already taken evasive action by dropping below the line of fire, and only the loudmouth was hit, cut down by enough lead to start a paperweight company.

Having blown their golden opportunity for an easy kill, the Iberian League assassins quickly corrected their aim for another go at blasting their elusive targets out of this world. Unfortunately for the terrorists, the Stony Man five were reluctant to make the journey and stated their feelings on the matter by unleashing the fury of their own weapons upon their terrorist foes.

One of the first killers to clock out of the game bought his ticket to nowhere via a short furious ride on McCarter's MAC-10 express. The doomed soul trapped on the wrong end of the Cockney's Ingram twitched and jerked in place as the Briton's bullets pelted his body. He finally slumped to the courtyard after McCarter set his sights on another likely prospect.

Yakov Katzenelenbogen's Uzi cut across the chest of a gun-toting killer and reversed, then swept to the right for a repeat performance on the next terrorist in line. Neither gunman knew what hit him, but they found out the hard way the drawback of a busted heart.

The .357 Desert Eagle in Gary Manning's fist spit fire twice, and another ambusher went down, nursing a spouting hole in his gut. Manning fired again, and a second hole joined the first, throwing the terrorist to the courtyard in a fit of swirling pain.

The man whom Calvin James pegged took his final curtain call, virtually cut in two by a hot line of lead. A long scream issued from his throat, and he slip-slid to death in a puddle of his own making.

Knowing he had come dangerously close to being killed by the very ones whom he had been clandestinely working with all along, Diaz felt no remorse delivering a trio of 9 mm slugs into the face of the last IL attacker. As the shots struck home, the terrorist's jaw shattered, his forehead caved in and his nose disintegrated. The gunman's legs kept the body going for another five feet, then folded at the knees and pitched the corpse into a scraping dive to the ground.

The staccato sound of gunfire was still hanging in the air when a second wave of Iberian League killers appeared in the villa's doorway. Concerned with the prospect of putting Phoenix Force on ice, they failed to notice the ball-shaped M-33 fragmentation grenade McCarter sent sailing their way.

The M-33 passed over their heads and dropped behind them inside the villa, exploding after two seconds, catching the terrorists completely off guard. Screams filled the night, and death, as blood and limbs were spewed on the courtyard.

"Green light and nothing to declare," McCarter announced, leaping to his feet and charging across the courtyard, jumping over the broken bodies cluttering the doorway as he dashed into the villa.

With the Briton covering their advance, the remaining Phoenix Force members, and finally Diaz, joined the Cockney inside the building. Beyond the doorway was a tile-covered corridor with doors leading left and right. The commandos moved down the hall and discovered both rooms in question—a den and a ground-level bedroom—to be deserted.

The end of the hallway veered to the right, but rather than risk exposing himself to enemy fire, McCarter tested conditions around the corner by tossing a half-empty pack of Player's cigarettes into the open. Immediately the end of the corridor was punctuated with a barrage of IL lead.

McCarter waited for the shooting to fade and, when it did, lobbed another M-33 far around the corner and into the center of the villa's living room. Someone shouted and swore in Spanish, and there was the crashing sound of furniture being overturned. Then the grenade exploded, and the shouts of fear and anger were transformed to high-pitched squeals.

McCarter stole a glance to assess the damage the M-33 had caused, then motioned for the others to follow as he swept around the corner like a cat on the prowl. The villa's front room had been reduced to a scrap pile. The lacerated remains of a couple of Iberian League terrorists had spattered the walls with streaks of red.

Three chairs and a sofa were splinters and sawdust. A statue of Cupid had been knocked from its pedestal, as though it tried wingless flight. Both the room's windows had lost their glass, while the curtains covering them were tattered shreds.

Double doors at the back of the room opened onto an unoccupied dining room dominated by an oak table large enough to seat a dozen or more. A staircase next to the double doors led upstairs. Before anyone set foot on the steps, though, a fresh herd of terrorists came thundering down in a charge preceded by their blazing submachine guns.

Knowing that the grenade-ravaged living room was no place for a violent confrontation, the Stony Man five and their reluctant companion, Diaz, separated and sought temporary refuge in opposite directions. Katz, McCarter and Diaz ducked into the dining room area, while James, Encizo and Manning hightailed it back into the main hallway.

The gunmen reached the bottom of the stairs and surged into the villa's living room, their SMGs wreaking havoc all the way. Then one of them noticed the room was empty, and he shouted above the din made by his comrades to stop shooting.

"The cowardly dogs have run away!" one of them proclaimed in disgust.

Just then Encizo and James appeared side by side to prove the man wrong, both Phoenix Force veterans triggering their weapons with a calm cool precision the IL killers would have appreciated had they lived long enough to remember the Cuban/American surprise. Manning took up the chorus with his .357 Eagle, and then McCarter and Katz joined in, trapping the savages herded together in a cross-fire web of destruction.

Annoyed for the second time that the Iberian League terrorists were still making no distinction between himself and the five gangsters from the United States, Diaz felt a macabre pleasure as he hosed down his Spanish allies with his Z-62 submachine gun. As the last of the gunmen collapsed to the floor, Diaz broke from his hiding place and took to the stairs, his flying feet taking the steps two and three at a time.

"What the hell?" James commented out loud. "What'd Diaz do . . . swallow a whole bottle of brave pills?"

"Nobody seems to be trying to pick him off," Manning said as the sound of the *comisario*'s pounding feet grew more faint. "Let's see what he's up to."

Diaz had been informed earlier in the evening how many Iberian League soldiers were assigned to Mantanez, and he'd tried to keep a head count of those who had been eliminated. He was almost willing to bet his life that all the men stationed at the villa were dead, but in the heat of battle, he could have miscounted. But he had to take that gamble because he had witnessed how poorly Mantanez reacted under pressure, and the last thing he needed was for the baldheaded wine merchant to be taken prisoner. Mantanez would sell his soul and implicate Diaz if he thought it would save his hide. The only way to prevent that from happening was to get to Mantanez ahead of the others.

Reaching the third-floor landing, Diaz went unerringly to Mantanez's hideaway and forced open the door by slamming against it with his shoulder while turning the doorknob. The door opened with a crash, and José Mantanez cried out in alarm as Diaz burst into the room.

"Oh, thank God it is you!" Mantanez, sitting in his chair with his hands clenched, was on the verge of tears. "All that shooting. All that noise. All I could think of was how I didn't want to die tonight." Mantanez frowned. "Why don't you speak?"

Instead of answering, Diaz squeezed the trigger of his Z-62 submachine gun and sprinkled the front of the older man's chest with a shower of 9 mm bullets. The brunt of the blast hit Mantanez like a runaway train, making him throw his hands into the air and totter back. The chair tipped over and dumped him on the floor.

"What happened?" Katz demanded as he entered the room.

Diaz pointed to Mantanez. "I had to shoot him after he went for a gun."

The Israeli looked down to the body at their feet. "I don't see any gun. Did you?"

"Not really," Diaz said defensively as the remaining members of the Phoenix Force crowded into the room.

"What's up?" Manning asked.

Katz pointed to the floor. "Meet Señor Mantanez. Diaz shot him because he thought Mantanez was reaching for a gun."

"An honest mistake," Diaz said. "It could happen to anyone."

"Not this time, mister," Katz amended sternly. "Why didn't you wait for us? Why the big hurry to get upstairs?"

"No hurry," Diaz said. "You and your men performed so courageously this evening that I felt obliged to follow your example."

"Right," Katz said, unconvinced. "Thanks for nothing. Mantanez was our sole link to the brains behind the Iberian League, and you just put him on ice."

"Maybe not," James corrected, kneeling beside Mantanez's body and feeling for a pulse. "Don't ask me how, but the dude is still breathing."

"What?" Diaz exclaimed, louder than necessary.

Mantanez groaned, and his eyes blinked open. His lips parted, letting a single bubble of blood escape. He made strange sounds. His eyes widened and focused on Diaz, then he gestured feebly with his index finger for James to lean forward to receive his dying message.

James listened carefully to the few words Mantanez spoke, then a terrible shudder ran through the wounded Spaniard and he was dead. James stood and promptly aimed his M-76 in Diaz's direction.

"Surprise. Surprise," James said. "Mantanez just told me you're with the Iberian League."

"Ridiculous!" Diaz said as Encizo disarmed him. "The man was obviously deranged and out of his mind."

"We'll be the judge of that," Katz advised.

23

Somewhere around two in the morning, at the U.S. consul general's office in Barcelona, Diaz was unable to resist the convincing effects of scopolamine, and promptly cranked out a tune that shot straight to the top of the charts. Diaz had never fancied himself much of a singer, but once Calvin James began the intense Q&A session, the Cuerpo General de Policía lieutenant colonel gave a wholehearted performance that answered all of Phoenix Force's questions.

Diaz's initial involvement with the Iberian League had a familiar ring to it: it began with heavy debts and expensive tastes and a salary unable to cope with either, and ended with a telephone call in the middle of the night that set up the first meeting between him and his IL bosses. Unlike many of those signing on with the terrorist organization, Diaz's commitment to the Iberian League was directly related to the balance in his bank account. So long as the Iberian League was willing to pay, Diaz was willing to play.

When asked who besides the late José Mantanez had helped put the IL package together, Diaz couldn't rattle off the names of Fernando Campos and Eduardo Vera fast enough. And he provided the reason behind forming the Iberian League. Just like Diaz, they were in it for the money: the three Spanish businessmen had determined to achieve Spain's withdrawal from the Common Market by whatever means possible in order to preserve the economic monopoly their products had enjoyed for generations. Spain's joining the EEC and the twentieth century didn't fit into their fiscal plans, but with the Iberian League working on their behalf, the terrorist organization's leaders fully expected it to be business as usual for them in the not too distant future.

Phoenix Force knew where José Mantanez could be found, but didn't know about Campos and Vera. No problem there, Diaz told them. The two ringleaders had temporarily departed from Madrid with the last of the IL soldiers to relocate in Córdoba at the José Mantanez estate in the event that Mantanez failed to stop Phoenix Force in Seville.

When questioned about the number of terrorists Campos and Vera had backing them up in Córdoba, the estimates Diaz came up with ran anywhere from twenty to forty men. The exact figure was difficult to pinpoint, given the flood of casualties suffered by the Iberian League during the past couple of days.

Once they had all the information they felt Diaz could supply, Phoenix Force left the *comisario* in the custody of Seville's U.S. consul general and a pair of no-nonsense MPs called in from Moron air base forty miles southeast of the city.

"Keep our prisoner under lock and key until you hear from us," Katz instructed the consul and the two military policemen. "In the meantime," the Israeli added, "my associates and I have urgent business to attend to. We thank you for your help."

"WE STILL HAVEN'T HEARD from José," Fernando Campos quietly commented to Eduardo Vera. "With each passing minute I am inclined to think we won't ever hear from him. Between you and me, Eduardo, I believe our dear friend, José, is dead."

Vera, his white hair a sharp contrast to the dark blue suit he wore, found it impossible to disagree. "My instincts speak the same message, Fernando. I no longer feel José to be among the living. And if his life has been snuffed out, then what of the lives of the men we sent with him? Surely, they have shared whatever fate has visited upon José?"

"Undoubtedly." Campos folded his hands together and sighed. "If José and the others are lost to us, it could mean we are the next to die."

"Why should that be?" Vera asked. "If José is gone, and wasn't questioned before his life came to an end, then the odds are in our favor that he carried the secret of our ties to the Iberian League with him to his grave. As for the others we sent to protect him, if one has died, then they all have died. The five men seeking to topple our Iberian League have done nothing by half measures since coming to Spain; it is unlikely they would start in Seville. Which is just as well for us because that leaves no one to lead the five devils to us."

"I sincerely trust you are right, Eduardo."

"So do I."

"In any case, it is good that we have come to Córdoba," Campos reflected. "If somehow our enemies have discovered our identities, then it is preferable we take a stand to defeat them on property owned by José, instead of someplace belonging to us. That way, should the authorities find need to investigate the matter later, there will be nothing to steer the police in our direction."

"Speaking of which," Vera said, "I think, once this business with the troublemakers from the United States has cooled down, we should seriously consider severing our relationship with Diaz. For what he has cost us to date, his performance on our behalf has been less than expected. I sincerely feel we could do better elsewhere."

"I agree one hundred percent," Campos said. "Let us take care of our five adversaries from America, and then we shall see about demonstrating to Diaz the virtues of early retirement. Diaz is a loose end to this entire miserable affair that we won't want dangling around." Campos rose from his chair and stretched. "It has been a long night. I will be glad to see the sunrise. I always feel more vulnerable in the dark."

"I do, as well," Vera said, "but in this instance I find myself surprisingly calm. With all the Iberian League soldiers we brought with us from Madrid, I doubt we have anything to fear."

Campos nodded. "Believe me, Eduardo, I hope you are right."

GARY MANNING ADJUSTED THE FOCUS of the Lowlight Miniscope as he surveyed the grounds of the expansive Cordoban estate. Engineered for clear vision and distortion-free resolution in starlight conditions, the second-generation Miniscope was also equipped with an infrared laser illuminator mounted coaxially on the device to provide additional illumination if required.

From his vantage point on a hill looking down on his objective, Manning slowly swept the Lowlight Miniscope from left to right, easily picking out the numerous Iberian League soldiers scattered in and about the estate. The majority of the Spanish terrorists the Canadian saw were gathered outside a two-story house. More enemy gunmen were hidden among a grove of olive trees.

Manning tucked the Miniscope away, then retreated several feet back down the hill to relay his observations to the rest of his team. "The info Diaz gave us was right on the money. Maybe our friends from the Iberian League aren't expecting us, but they're sure as hell geared up for a fight if one comes."

"Good," McCarter said. "We wouldn't want to disappoint them."

"How many gunmen are there?" Katz wanted to know.

"I counted twenty-five," Manning replied, then went on to detail the areas where each group of terrorists was concentrated.

"What about Campos and Vera?" Encizo asked after Manning had finished. "Any sign of them?"

Manning shook his head. "But that doesn't automatically mean they're off sawing logs. There's a light shining through one of the windows in the house, so that could be them. If they've been up all night waiting for a call from Mantanez, then I doubt they've had much sleep."

"They can join the club," James said, rubbing his eyes. "From Madrid to Barcelona to Valencia and back to Madrid, then down to Seville and out to Moron air base for the shuttle flight here to Córdoba. After a while you start feeling like a pinball who's never heard of the word *tilt*."

"Don't remind me," Katz said, still recovering from the turbulent air ride from Seville.

"What's our plan, Katz?" Manning asked.

"Basically this," the Israeli answered. "We'll get into position and then—" he pointed to the dark outline of a hill behind them "—wait for the sun to come creeping over that hill. This will put the sun right in the Iberian League's eyes, and make it that much harder for them to see us when we attack."

"Not that they won't have other things to think about," James said, indicating a large canvas duffel bag at his feet. "Once the babies I brought start flying, it's going to be Chicken Little time on the hacienda. Our IL compadres will think the sky's falling in on them for sure."

"True," Yakov Katzenelenbogen agreed. "But that's their problem."

DAWN DEVOURED THE NIGHT, and the early morning sun pushed its face over the crest of the hill to the east of the estate. Watching the sunrise from a window at the front of the house, Campos squinted against the increasing brightness and turned away to where Vera sat comfortably reading a newspaper.

"Morning at last," Campos said with relief. "And still no telephone call from José."

"Yet we had no nocturnal visit from our five persistent opponents, either," Vera said, folding his paper. "We get the good with the bad. It's what gives life balance."

"I wouldn't know about that," Campos said, "but..." He stopped talking in midsentence as a distant rumble shook the house. "What was that?"

"Thunder?" Vera guessed.

"Impossible!" Campos said, spinning back around to the window. "There's not a cloud in the sky."

Vera joined Campos at the window as a second growling vibration rattled the house, and an olive tree and the two IL soldiers standing beside it in the grove nearby vanished in a terrible explosion.

"My God!" gasped Campos. "They are here! We're under attack!"

It was clear by then that Campos was stating the obvious.

Calvin James had gotten the early-morning assault rolling by launching the first of a dozen SLAM rounds into the air and onto the estate occupied by the Iberian League forces. The SLAM, a silent mortar designed by Napco International, fired noiseless, flashless, smokeless ammunition. It resembled the Japanese "knee mortar" of World War II and had a maximum range of six hundred meters.

While James could have caused more damage with the SLAM launcher if he had taken longer to recalculate each shot, his primary purpose for utilizing Napco's pride and joy was to disorient and frighten the enemy, a tactic, judging from the cries of alarm and confusion coming from the estate, that worked.

As he completed launching the last of his silent rounds, James traded the SLAM for his M-76 submachine gun, then went charging over the top of the hill to confront his IL foes head-on. Autofire in the distance told him his teammates had already met up with the enemy, prompting the warrior from Chicago to move faster. Sloppy seconds had never been his style.

Emptying his lungs in a hideous scream of despair, a dumbfounded terrorist stared in disbelief at his gun, which was lying in the dirt. The fallen weapon wasn't the problem: what had initiated the hysteria was the man's amputated hand still clutching the gun. Then a follow-up SLAM round dropped onto the wounded killer, and his troubles disappeared.

"What's happening?" a confused terrorist shouted amid the seemingly endless series of explosions that left no part of the estate untouched. Off to his right, someone yelled at him, and he turned, reacting without thinking and firing his SMG into the face of one of his comrades. Dead on his feet, the headless Iberian Leaguer spilled to the ground, and his murderer dropped to his knees and was violently sick.

That wasn't the single instance of that careless mistake. As the SLAM rounds virtually seemed to drop out of nowhere, most of the terrorists were reduced to running around in mindless circles, ready to shoot anything that moved.

The rising sun at their backs, the men of Phoenix Force surged forward to the attack, asking no quarter and giving none. Their targets were savages who willingly slaughtered innocent tourists, and the rewards for bringing the terrorists to justice were immeasurable to the Stony Man five.

Unleashing the fury of their weapons as they struck at the heart of the Iberian League stronghold, Phoenix Force had the grim satisfaction of seeing their adversaries' resolve disappear under the devastating suddenness of the strike. In a matter of seconds, the Cordoban estate became an open-air morgue. Bodies of the dead and dying were everywhere, littering the grounds of the Spanish plantation with rampant death and destruction.

Sensing a rush of movement down a hillside to their left, two gunmen whirled sideways, only to find themselves blinded by the rising sun stinging their eyes and unable to properly aim their Z-62 submachine guns. Triggering their SMGs in a desperate effort to save their lives, their random shots failed to stop Calvin James or to alter the effectiveness of his Smith & Wesson M-76. Struck by multiple 9 mm parabellum rounds, the doomed pair hit the dirt and played dead for keeps.

The last of the SLAM surprises launched by James hadn't yet fallen when Manning and Encizo stormed to the side of the house. They were immediately confronted by four terrorists dashing around the corner. Encizo's MP-5 sputtered to life, and like angry hornets the death-dealers converged on one of the terrorists. The man opened his mouth for a scream that never emerged as the mouth snapped shut in silent surrender.

The terrorist nearest Manning frantically wielded his weapon to fire at point-blank range on the Canadian's chest, but Manning beat him to the punch. Deflecting the rifle over and down with his left hand, he extended his right to grip the .357 Eagle and squeezed off a couple of shots. One Magnum rocket shattered the gunman's lower jaw, while the second .357 slug shrouded his neck in a geyser of blood.

The killer collapsed, but in the grip of death he managed to pull the trigger of his assault rifle and send a bullet plowing into the foot of the terrorist beside him. Distracted by the river of pain flowing up his leg, the hood only had time to register from the corner of his eye that Encizo's H&K machine pistol was leveled on him, then ended his agony forever.

One of the terrorists was still on his feet and unloosed a staccato hail that slammed into the wall behind Encizo, then Manning fired again and made it a clean sweep across the board. Manning's bullet blasted through the gunman's heart, and he slumped against the wall to slide to the ground, leaving red streaks on the white paint.

With their universe disintegrating before their eyes, Campos and Vera backed away from the window to contemplate their next move. In each man's hand was a Star M-28 9 mm autoloader. The two ringleaders had armed themselves once the fighting got underway.

"Our men are useless," Campos concluded with disgust. "They're not doing a damn thing to protect the estate, let alone you and me."

"That's because they are too preoccupied with dying," Vera said. "It is time to admit defeat, Fernando. We're finished. The Iberian League is through.''

"Never!" Campos raised his voice, his eyes flicking nervously to the window as the noise of the conflict drew closer. "There must be a way out for us, an avenue we haven't thought of."

"None of our plans ever included an emergency escape route," Vera said. "We were too sure of ourselves, and now it is too late. We can let them take us, or we can fight and die. Either way our honor is history."

"Don't say that!" Campos shouted, then pointed excitedly to the window. "Look, coming across the yard toward the house. It is the old one-armed one who has repeatedly outsmarted us at every turn."

"I see him," Vera said, noting that another of the enemy soldiers had joined the gray-haired man. "And he is not alone." Vera lifted his Star M-28 into the air. "I'm sorry, Fernando, but I can't let them capture me. At my age, the shame of public humiliation would be unbearable. Our dream was good while it lived, but now it has deserted us. Farewell, my friend."

And with that, Eduardo Vera limped back to the window and began firing his handgun straight through the glass at his approaching targets.

Katz and McCarter were twenty-five feet away when the large picture window at the front of the house was shattered by Eduardo Vera's bullets as the senior Iberian League boss endeavored to gun down the unit commander of Phoenix Force and Mrs. McCarter's favorite son. Vera's autoloader had a capacity for firing sixteen rounds, but less than a third of that number exited the chamber before Katz and McCarter retaliated.

Caught in a deadly cross fire, Vera's body blossomed tiny petals of red. His Star M-28 dropped from his fingers, and his face became a mask of pain. Katz and McCarter stopped firing, and Vera, his legs buckling under him, raised his hand as though in goodbye, then flashed his teeth and toppled backward out of sight.

"Diabolical," McCarter remarked. "The geezer smiled at us just as he was falling."

"That must have been Eduardo Vera," Katz said, sprinting with McCarter up to the house. "Which still leaves Fernando Campos to account for."

Manning and Encizo appeared from around a corner, and James showed up moments later. An unnatural calm had settled over the estate, in sharp contrast to the sounds of combat that had greeted the sunrise. Corpses littered the ground in every direction.

"What's the good word?" Encizo inquired.

"Fernando Campos," Katz answered. "We suspect he's the only one left."

Manning jerked his thumb at the house. "In there?"

"Yeah," Katz said.

"Well, if he's anything like the rest of his mates," McCarter decided, "he's got a gun ready to use on us the second we step inside." McCarter withdrew an M-26 grenade and said, "Let's take the easy road for a change. Back in a tick."

The Cockney left them, and, keeping low, crept underneath the bullet-blasted window. He pulled the grenade's safety pin and heaved the M-26 into the house. The Londoner was four seconds into his retreat to his friends when the fragmentation grenade exploded with a roar, stinging the ears as chunks of stone were gouged from the house. Fernando Campos was bodily launched through the window, then crashed headfirst to the ground, his neck at an awkward angle.

"Way to go!" Encizo congratulated McCarter.

"Pure luck," Manning observed.

"Talent," McCarter corrected.

"All that counts is that the Iberian League is finished," Katz said.

"And now we can go home," James added. "Spain's a beautiful country, but I think I'd scream if we had to travel to one more Spanish city."

"Me, too," McCarter grinned. "Holy Toledo!"

DON PENDLETON'S EXECUTIONER

MACK BOLAN™

Baptized in the fire and blood of Vietnam, Mack Bolan has become America's supreme hero. Fiercely patriotic and compassionate, he's a man with a high moral code whose sense of right and wrong sometimes violates society's rules. In adventures filled with heart-stopping action, Bolan has thrilled readers around the world. Experience the high-voltage charge as Bolan rallies to the call of his own conscience in daring exploits that place him in peril with virtually every heartbeat.

"Anyone who stands against the civilized forces of truth and justice will sooner or later have to face the piercing blue eyes and cold Beretta steel of Mack Bolan...civilization's avenging angel."
— *San Francisco Examiner*

Mack Bolan's

by Dick Stivers

Action writhes in the reader's own streets
as Able Team's Carl "Ironman" Lyons,
Pol Blancanales and Gadgets Schwarz
make triple trouble in blazing war. Join
Dick Stivers's Able Team as it returns to
the United States to become the country's
finest tactical neutralization squad in an
era of urban terror and unbridled crime.

"Able Team will go anywhere, do anything,
in order to complete their mission. Plenty
of action! Recommended!"
—*West Coast Review of Books*

GOLD EAGLE

Able Team titles are available
wherever paperbacks are sold.

AT-1

Take
4 explosive books
plus a
mystery bonus
FREE

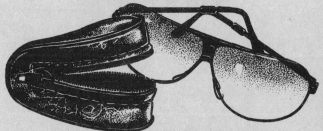